It's about Luke

Gwenyth Snow

For Bonnie

Thank you for coming. It's always a pleasure to see you.

 FriesenPress

Suite 300 - 990 Fort St
Victoria, BC, V8V 3K2
Canada

www.friesenpress.com

Copyright © 2018 by Gwenyth Snow
First Edition — 2018

Edited by Irene Kavanagh

Medical Consultant: Dr. Lyle McGonigle

Although some of the situations and characters have been pulled from real life experiences, this work is a piece of fiction. Names, characters, places, events and incidents have been changed to protect the innocent.

All rights reserved.

No part of this publication may be reproduced in any form, or by any means, electronic or mechanical, including photocopying, recording, or any information browsing, storage, or retrieval system, without permission in writing from FriesenPress.

ISBN
978-1-5255-2057-0 (Hardcover)
978-1-5255-2058-7 (Paperback)
978-1-5255-2059-4 (eBook)

1. FICTION, FAMILY LIFE

Distributed to the trade by The Ingram Book Company

For David....

....who always knew that difference defines us and acceptance completes us.

Acknowledgments

Although this book is fiction, one of the primary characters, David, is based on my own son who passed away just before his twentieth birthday. I want to thank the countless people and organizations involved in his care. His/our survival would have been impossible without them. While we never could have managed without the support we received, getting that support was often difficult. Wading through the bureaucratic maze of countless forms and phone numbers is a daunting, and often demoralizing, exercise. Thank you to those who try to make that process in any way easier for those of us who become overwhelmed.

This novel pulls from aspects of my life but it is not a memoir. One of the book's purposes is to reflect on the circumstances that envelop disability and care as a whole. In my experience, many mothers of disabled children handle the majority of the work and decisions on their own and in isolation. I want to tell the story from their point of view. However, I would like to acknowledge that my ex-husband, from whom I separated when David was a baby, nonetheless became a very big part of his life. David also had a strong relationship with his baba, dido, and cousin who showered him with love, attention, and respect.

I would like to thank June for always being there to support me through David's admissions into hospital – all fifty-six times.

I would like to thank Dr. L. McGonigle, pediatrician and friend, for reviewing the novel for medical accuracy.

A huge shout-out to my editor, Irene Kavanagh, whose expertise and advice has been invaluable.

Thanks to all the people in my life who encouraged, listened, suggested, and advised me throughout this lengthy process.

Finally, I'd like to recognize and applaud all the moms, dads, brothers and sisters who, like Luke, are often given a back seat to the needs and wants required by a family member with a disability. It's not enough to say you're not alone—but it's a start.

It's about

Luke

Prologue

No one should ever be too old for the comfort and security of a stuffed animal, even when no longer a child. If he had one right now he would have it shoved under his arm, unashamed, daring anyone to say something. You don't have to think when you're holding something; you just hug it, and it hugs you back, healing some of the raw damage that dangles inside. Grief has no boundaries, and does not exclude age, differences, or species. He didn't know how to feel, but he was certain of one thing: if there were any sad memories or thoughts trying to cloud his mind, he'd be better equipped to clear them with something to hug.

Chapter 1
Celebrating (Edmonton, Alberta, 2002)

The heartache Luke Poole felt contradicted the satisfying warmth of the sun that shone on his face through the car window. He sat quietly in the moving sedan, headed for the gathering to honour families of disabled children who had died. He closed his eyes to embrace the healing sensation as he drew in shallow breaths. The invitation lay stiffly in his hand: a dark-brown card, decorated with a string of beads and a small piece of twig. The text at the top read, "A Spiritual Gathering: In Celebration of Life and Death for Families and Caregivers Grieving the Death of a Child. Saturday, October 14, 2002."

Clutching the card, he opened his eyes and came face to face with his own reflection in the window glass. His eyes looked round and deep-set, marked by a slant of sadness. His nose was narrow, and his mouth was set firmly in a determined line. Straight, brown hair hung slightly over his ears, and his bangs were swept carelessly across his forehead. In one week he would be twelve, and it would be a month since the tragedy that had profoundly impacted his life. As he stared through the window, his mind drifted off…until he felt a tug. She never said a word, but held his hand gently against the side of her skirt, the dark material cool and soft against his skin.

As the car slowed near the corner of a familiar street, he looked up at the majestic house he had visited on more than one occasion. He and Mother, with David, his nearly thirteen-year old disabled brother, had volunteered many times to help with these celebrations, which occurred every few years. This was the home of Dr. Francis Liam, the pediatrician who had looked after him and David from the beginning of their lives.

She whispered softly to him. "It'll be OK, Luke."

He reached for the door handle and exited onto the street. *How can it ever be OK?* But as he looked through the open gate into the yard prepared for some two hundred guests, he felt better. The large group of people circulating made him feel a little less alone in his lingering grief. He felt like he was about to enter Diagon Alley, from *Harry Potter*. He would leave one reality and enter another, which was often overlooked by the "Muggles" of the dominant society. Although the magic in this world was of a different sort, and nowhere near as much fun as that of Potter's world. He advanced toward the crowd and felt the uneasiness of transition, like Harry did on platform nine and three quarters at King's Cross station.

The expansive property housed Dr. Francis Liam and his family. He was well-known and highly respected, and his reputation had grown over the years due to his devotion, love, and skill. He was a pleasant-looking man in his fifties, with an air and appearance not unlike George Clooney's. Whip-smart, candid, and kind, he also had a short, Irish temper, and a manner often less than gentle. In professional circles, he was referred to as "stocky, cocky, and usually right." His large practice was dominated by children with highly complicated conditions, or extreme disabilities, and he was the primary reason why many flourished. Even after their deaths, he continued to be a part of their families' lives.

The house was a two-story dwelling with a solid front of stone and wood. Luke knew that the back of the house was mainly a wall of glass open to the untamed beauty of the birch trees, rocks, and moss that it nestled into comfortably. A narrow creek coursed through the entanglement of flora, passing a pond filled with red-and-white koi that slipped in and out of a thicket of water plants. Inside the house, an open stairway spiraled upward to the floor above, and twisted downward to the floor below. Every inch of wall space was covered with art obtained on various travels, gifted by numerous patients, or carefully chosen for the special memory or meaning it held for the family. The house stood as a living entity of its own, filled with life, love, and story.

At the front gate, Luke stood by the table of greeters, who welcomed guests and handed out name tags. Tables filled with pastries, fruit, cheese, and biscuits, large urns of coffee and tea, and jugs of juice lined the edge of the driveway. Further into the yard, the three-car garage stayed open and empty, except for an expansive rectangular table that spread across the front like the open wings of an eagle. The table's edge was lined with a hundred cylindrical candles, each wrapped with a strap of leather, or thong. Each thong held a single swatch of tanned leather embellished with the words, "Lend me the stone strength of the past and I will lend you the wings of the future." Small feathers and beads decorated each leather swatch, and the down feathers puffed up, as if they had breath, when the air stirred. A row of a hundred potted orchids stood behind the candles. The tall stems and delicate yellow blossoms arched over, as if performing graceful dives. Chairs had been set up in the driveway under a canopied tent to shield visitors from the bite of the sun's hot rays, or the sting of cold drops from dark clouds.

A film screen stood to one side of the fold-up chairs. A table and computer had been placed in front of it to display photos of the children from Dr. Liam's practice who had died over the past thirteen years. In the distance, along one side of the house, the peak of a teepee poked above the canopy of trees. Luke had visited it before, and knew it was there as a place for families to write messages to their loved ones, or to pray in private. Outside the teepee, a drummer sat in traditional Cree dress, pounding on a round, animal-skin drum. The sound replicated the rhythm of a child's heartbeat: quick, steady, strong. Dr. Liam was not aboriginal, but many aspects of aboriginal beliefs and customs blended well with his own, so he embraced them.

Luke looked around, and nodded to a few people, who waved in recognition. He averted his eyes to avoid the sadness in theirs. He did not want to talk, nor did he want anyone to touch him. He wanted to stay invisible, and experience the day without explanation or tears. He sat on a metal chair on an aisle and closed his eyes, taking in the aroma of burning sweet grass that drifted past as he waited. He thought about all the families there. The threat of death was not a stranger to them. Death had stalked his brother every day. As a family, they had lived day to day with that threat, never knowing if a cough would turn into something horrific, even lethal.

But this? He hadn't seen this coming. No one had seen it coming. His only comfort was that there were lots of fond memories to transform into good stories. He had many great stories, just like most of the people here. It was a day for stories—a day for sharing struggles, heartache, laughter…and especially, love.

Chapter 2
Moving (2000)

～～～～～

On a warm October afternoon, an ancient, dark-green van limped its way forward to the front of a bungalow-style home. The flower beds under the front windows were empty and dry. One large tree loomed on the edge of the lawn, its huge root base sucking the life from any other plants and grass that dared to grow. From outside, the house looked well-kept, if not inviting. It was ghost-like and almost invisible, with nothing remarkable about its structure or character except for the wide, cement sidewalk that sloped downward from the front door to the road, to accommodate a wheelchair.

Nine-year-old Luke, in ripped jeans and a Disney *Hercules* T-shirt, burst out of the passenger side of the van he affectionately referred to as Smog. He and Mother had named it after the dragon Smaug, from *The Hobbit*. They pronounced it smog, the way everyone did at the time, and it was a fitting name for the van. It was green, old, and puffed out large balls of smoke from the exhaust whenever starting or stopping. He leapt excitedly toward the double doors, pulling them open to reveal a grate. It fell with a whirring sound, opening like a drawbridge and stopping when flush with the van floor. David, who was older by a year, wiggled inside the straps that held him secure. As Mother pushed him onto the ramp, the sun caught the sparkle in his hair, and brightened the strikingly beautiful face beneath the blonde curls. His skin glowed, and his green eyes flashed like gems in the brightness. He laughed with delight as the ramp was lowered to the ground. He had been born with a severe form of cerebral palsy, a condition limiting him to such an extent that the only thing he could do independently was smile. But his smile warmed the earth.

The chair was an extension of him. His head was supported by a headrest, and a chest strap held him securely against the back of the chair. A fabric strap ran across his lap and fastened crossways with another clip that snapped together in the middle. Both his feet were strapped down onto foot pedals, to position them forward. A pummel between his legs kept his hips in a normal rotation, to prevent his legs from sagging inward. He was as secure as Fort Knox, but his spirit was not bound by straps or his condition. His arms and head had some free, although limited, movement. He smiled brightly to show his approval of leaving the van, but without independent speech, he could only squeal excitedly, while searching for the figure of his adoring brother.

"Can I push him?" Luke asked as he positioned himself behind David and reached for the handles that extended from the chair. David laughed as Luke grunted and pushed him a few feet forward. The chair curved sideways onto the grass and stuck. Mother impatiently guided Luke out of the way. She turned the chair, then steered David up the slope to the front door, setting both brakes on when they reached the top of the walk.

She glanced through the front window as she pushed her hair off her face. "I want you two to wait here until I get a path cleared through the living room. There are boxes everywhere, and I won't get David through the door until I make some room."

"But how long do we have to wait? I want to see what it looks like inside," Luke said. He jiggled his body impatiently, excited to explore their new home.

"Just be patient," Mother replied in a tight voice. "Give me ten seconds. Can you do that? And don't let the cats out." Her tone held a trace of annoyance that had nothing to do with Luke. Life had become more complicated and stressful. As she disappeared inside, Luke moved to the front of his brother's chair.

"Ten seconds! We wait ten seconds!"

David smiled in response, looking into his brother's eyes.

"*OK*, let's *cownt*," Luke said in his best Dracula accent. "Wuuun-anda-twoooooo-anda-thhhhreee!"

David startled to giggle.

"Fffffour! Fffffffiiiive! Sixseveneightnineten!"

David giggled harder. He fought for each breath, but couldn't take his eyes off of his brother's antics.

Luke fanned his fingers like a magician in front of David's face. "It eez time to *gohhh*!" he said dramatically.

Forgetting they were on an incline, Luke released one of the brakes. The chair tugged to one side. David's giggling stopped abruptly, and a startled look appeared on his face. He made a loud sound in protest. Luke reached for the other brake. David shrieked. As Luke grasped the second brake to pull it up, he heard a faint jingling sound, just before a woman's hand was laid gently over his.

June Littlechild often appeared as the calm in the wake of a storm. Of Cree heritage, she was Mother's fiercely loyal friend, and had been part of the boys' lives from the time they were born.

"Hey, Star Wars," she said, using Luke's nickname, as she placed her body behind the chair. She unlocked the second brake, and maneuvered David safely through the doorway, balancing a cardboard tray with two coffees in the other hand. A slight grin showed on her thin, wide, lips. "I think you were about to send your brother for a bigger ride than you were expecting." She turned and pointed. "See how the sidewalk slants down to the street where the van is parked?"

Luke nodded.

"David's chair, with its anti-tippers, would have gone backwards down the sidewalk and smashed up against the side of the van."

Luke nodded again, envisioning the near disaster. "Oh." It was all he could say.

"You should be more careful with your brother. He's bendy, but he's breakable," June said, with the lingering further hint of a smile.

David reached out his hand in a jerky fashion, to slowly run his fingers through the long strands of June's hair, which fell to her waist. Her smooth, dark-brown tresses were tinted with reddish streaks, not unlike the colour of wild-cherry bark. Her skin, the colour of cream-lightened coffee, was highlighted by expressive, golden-brown eyes. She was in her mid-thirties, of average height and weight, and wore a loose, western-style blouse that hung over a long, cotton skirt. Tiny silver bells sewn into the skirt's hem made a tinkling sound when she moved. A beaded necklace with a large turquoise at its centre hung from around her neck. At her side, a mature, golden retriever stood patiently, his tail whipping from side to side like a windshield wiper. The large canine took no notice of the family cats, Bronte and Montgomery, now heading in the direction of the fish tank.

Luke spoke to the dog and playfully ruffled his ears. "Were you a good boy? Were you a good boy for Auntie?" he asked in the mock, childish tone often used with animals and babies.

Goliath thumped his large tail animatedly on the linoleum floor.

"Auntie? You think I'm the dog's aunt?" June asked.

"You're our auntie, so you're Goliath's auntie, too."

"Actually, I'm David's and your godmother, so Goliath will have to be happy with a godmother instead." She kissed the top of David's head. "Morning, Star Shine!" she said, taking in his beaming smile, the beauty of his face, and the delight in his eyes.

"June, is that you?" Mother asked as she emerged from another room, dusting off her hands. "You got here almost before we did. Mind you, your vehicle doesn't break down at every other street corner."

"Love your shirt," June said. Mother wore a boy's oversized T-shirt with an anime character on the front. Her clothing choice made it apparent that laundry was not an immediate priority.

Mother ignored the comment. "Just before you arrived, I was trying to clear some space to bring the boys into the living room." She stopped short when she noticed Luke. "I thought I told you to wait outside," she said in an accusatory tone.

"You said ten seconds. We waited ten seconds," said Luke.

"That's not what I meant. You should have waited till I told you to come in."

Luke turned so she couldn't see him roll his eyes.

Mother turned to June, trying to calm the annoyance in her voice. "Thanks so much for looking after Goliath. It was a big help to have him out of the way."

June winked at Luke. "He was no bother. Glad to see you got here OK and that the boys arrived *inside* safely."

"What do you mean by that?" Mother asked, catching the exchange between June and Luke.

"Well," June began cautiously, "the boys were alone on the landing. Luke was trying to be helpful, by taking David's brakes off so he could push him through the doorway. That could have sent him sailing backwards down the walk into the van parked by the curb. He could have been hurt."

Mother's mouth dropped open. A swift anger blew over her as she imagined the potential disaster. She aimed her venom at Luke, who shuffled his feet as he stood in front of the fish tank. "How could you be so careless?" The words snapped off her tongue.

"*Nitotem*," June said, using the Cree word for friend, "he was just trying to get his brother inside. That's all."

Once it was out of her mouth, she realized she had said too much. In a gesture of kindness, she held out a hot cup of Tim Hortons' coffee. "One milk, one Splenda?" she asked, grinning sheepishly.

"Oh, so what you're saying is that it wouldn't have been his fault, but would have been mine?"

"No," June said, "but I think you have to be a few jumps ahead of our friend Skywalker. He's just a boy."

"But I'm going to have to depend on him more. This situation we are in isn't just about him!" Mother said, feeling insulted.

"I know, but he's only nine. David is a huge responsibility."

Mother raised her hands, palms outward. "So what am I supposed to do? Our situation was tough enough with two incomes and a handful of help. Now it's down to me. My husband has gone missing—but there's no evidence of foul play, according to the police. No word, just gone, with most of the money from our bank account. We've had to move and change schools in less than a month."

Her emotions bubbled to the surface, and she tried to calm herself by turning her attention to stacked boxes. There was one on the floor overflowing with various VHS tapes that she knew the boys loved. Four other boxes were labelled "Books." The tops were sealed to keep them closed, and their contents free from damage. Several more boxes contained medical supplies, feeding bags, packages of incontinent briefs, wound care, limb supports, soaker pads, and other necessary needs for David's care. There were more than a dozen boxes and bags for those things alone.

She pulled out two black plastic garbage bags marked "clothes" from the never-ending piles of boxes, one bag labeled "David," and the other "Luke." She tossed David's into the largest bedroom, which they would share, and the other into the smallest room.

June watched, and considered her answer to Mother's question. "This isn't anyone's fault," she finally said, "especially not the boys. I guess one thing you can do is pray to the spirits, and hope they're on your side."

"Oh, that's real helpful—spirits. Like that's going to do something," Mother replied sarcastically.

She turned to look at a few pieces of furniture that seemed abandoned in the living room, trying to decide where to place them and which boxes to empty first. She felt overwhelmed, a common feeling of late. "I'm just so tired. My shifts are long, and David wakes every two hours at night because he needs something. It's all physical. *Everything* I do takes energy that I don't have…everything." She scowled at her coffee cup. Even drinking felt like work.

David made a series of bird noises and delighted sounds. A broad smile emerged on his face, and a chuckle surfaced from his throat. He sat looking up at the large picture window.

"Well, at least somebody's happy," June said in a light voice.

David had seen a red spider hanging from a spot on the curtain rod. It turned and twisted in the light, the reflection making the nearly invisible thread sparkle as the tiny inhabitant moved quickly up and down, creating its new home. Luke, June, and Mother assembled at his side. They watched in silent awe as the creature worked its magic, creating its space and place in the universe.

June felt that the wonder of this tiny creature was much like the wonder of this family. Their value could be easily missed, and their uniqueness overlooked. She smiled at the spider, and patted David's head in gratitude for drawing her attention to the inspiration that might have passed unnoticed. She took another sip of coffee. "You don't miss a thing, do you, David?"

He made a bird sound, not unlike a sparrow, and continued watching the crimson spider dancing in the light.

After a few hours of emptying boxes, the living room had taken better shape with the few pieces of furniture, including a small TV, arranged in the cramped space. A wooden pedestal with an aquarium perched on top stood to the left of the television. Luke watched his goldfish swim lazily through the plastic reeds and around the pump.

"Cowabunga, dude!" He grumbled the favourite phrase from *Teenage Mutant Ninja Turtles* as he poked a finger at the glass where the pink goldfish swam. She was a birthday present from the year before, christened Princess Leia by Mother. He watched the fish move gracefully through the water, winding in and out of the tufts of plastic reeds. He loved fish. He loved their movement, grace, and special natures, but he would have preferred a Siamese fighting fish, or a lionfish, or something a little more dangerous-looking. David got a dog named Goliath, a big protective dog that wouldn't hurt a fly (although no one would know that at first glance). All he got was a silly little fish, and having a pink, girly fish named Leia was a huge embarrassment for anyone, let alone someone whose name was Luke.

"It's starting to rain!" June said. She took an empty box, flattened it, and stacked it against the collection of garbage bags at the back door. "Luke, could you come help me take this stuff out to the trash before I go?"

Luke pulled himself away from the fish tank and walked to the back door, passing David watching TV. "How come you never have to do anything? Why is it always me?" he grumbled.

"Luke, are you coming?"

He sighed and pulled on his boots. "Yes."

"Are you working tomorrow?" June asked Mother as she reached for the door handle.

"I was scheduled to, but the hospital called and said I didn't have to come in. It's making me nervous. That's the third time this month."

"I heard the same thing from Maria and Lilly," June said. "Seems to be happening all over, but don't worry about it too much right now. Luke and I are heading out to the garbage. Then I'll be on my way."

"Thanks for your help," Mother responded. "I'll call you later."

June and Luke headed for the garbage bin at the end of the lot. He scanned the tightly packed complex of buildings. Children of different races ran and played in the parking lot, and there were even a few about his age.

"You think you're going to be OK here?" June asked. "It's quite a different neighbourhood from where you were."

"Sure, we'll be fine," he said, watching a young girl run past with her tongue out and her middle finger up.

"You need anything…you call me. Promise?"

"Promise." He set the trash to the side of the overflowing bin, and watched as two police officers approached the front door of a townhouse. One officer knocked while the other stood aside, gun raised.

This was going to be a serious change from what he knew.

Chapter 3
Splashing

Later that afternoon, Mother got the boys ready to walk to the grocery store, several blocks away. It was raining heavily, and Smog wouldn't start. Mother dressed the boys in waterproof pants, jackets, and boots. Rain or no rain, they needed groceries, or they would be sharing food with the felines. She pushed David's chair from the back of the house and into the parking lot. Hours of heavy rain had created a minefield of puddles, which spread across the black tar and seemed to summon Luke and his yellow gum boots. He dashed toward a small puddle, and Mother's voice boomed behind him.

"Luke, stop! We're going to get wet enough as it is without you making it worse. Come on, hold on to David's chair. You know better than to run through puddles. It'll make you sick, and I don't have time for that."

Luke's head dropped. He dragged his boots alongside the chair as the trio began their exit out of the parking lot. He watched David lift his face into the rain, flinching as the drops landed, and squirming with delight at the tickling feeling.

An elderly, sad-faced woman, wearing a rain hat and transparent galoshes, locked her eyes on David as she approached, and stopped in front of his chair. "Oh, mercy! You poor, wee thing—to have to go through so much. I'm so sorry this has happened to you." She grabbed both of his hands and started to shake them up and down. "What's wrong with him?" she asked Mother, her voice edged with sympathy.

"He was born prematurely and has cerebral palsy," Mother replied automatically.

"Oh, my! Did you drink or smoke? Did you have a decent doctor? Maybe you did something bad in another life?"

Mother stood dumbstruck. Was she actually being blamed? She usually let such statements pass, with the realization that some people didn't get it and would never get it. But this time, this day, she had no patience left.

"Sometimes things just happen without anyone or anything to blame," she said impatiently. "And even if there were, what's the point?"

Undeterred, the woman continued. "Such a shame that he'll never experience so many things, like playing football, or riding a bike, or even just splashing in a mud puddle. A shame. A true shame!"

She ended the exchange, patting David on the hand. "God bless," she said with a sad smile, and went on her way.

Luke waited for Mother to regain their pace. *Why is she standing so still?*

She began to mimic the old woman. "Such a shame he won't experience things!" she said in an exaggerated voice. "Such a shame, such a *shame*! Bless *me*? Blast *you*, y'old bat!"

She slammed on David's brakes, and then, as if on a mission, undid in quick succession the myriad of straps that held her son secure in his chair. She pulled him forward and stood him up, balancing his back against her. His upper body could not support itself, which prevented him from sitting independently, but his legs could move quickly when he wanted them to. She held his torso against her body, and with his legs pumping like a smoothly operating machine, moved him into the puddle. His legs raced ahead as she tried to catch him up with his body.

Luke stood and watched. He had been chastised for the doing the very thing David was now doing. He didn't understand how or why, but he sensed the unfairness of it all. David's boots went into the puddle. Mother bounced him up and down in the water, and he whooped and hollered as they jumped through the puddles. David's joyful enthusiasm became infectious, and Luke began to abandon his feeling of hurt. The more David shouted, the more he wanted to join in. He jumped into an adjacent puddle, and felt the thrill of getting soaked beside Mother and David while they blissfully made a spectacle of themselves.

Mother grew exhausted from holding David. She plopped him down in the puddle and took a deep breath as she balanced him against her legs.

"Take that, you old busybody! How *dare* you blame me, or God, or anyone else!"

The boys looked at her, Luke shrugged and then they went back to splashing and making themselves happy.

Chapter 4
Gifting

~~~~~

The following day, June waited on the sidewalk for Smog to limp up and Mother to unload David at the front of the mall. Mother and Luke's appointment would allow David to go shopping. He seemed excited and pleased to see June.

As she guided him and his cumbersome chair into a department store, June ignored the stares and frowning faces. As an aboriginal, she was not a stranger to being stared at. Nor were she and David strangers to planned outings together. She could imagine the thoughts running through others' minds. *Is she his mother? How did she contribute to his disability? How much money does she get for looking after him?*

She parked the chair beside the store-location chart and began reading the shop names. "OK, Boo," she said. The nickname had surfaced after playing peek-a-boo, a game David loved when he was younger. "There's Dungeon and Dragons."

She looked at him, but he showed no reaction.

"How about Hats and More? We could get Luke a baseball cap for his birthday!"

There was still no reaction.

"Kites and Models? ... Hoodies, Tees and Jeans?...HMV?...Pets 'n' U?"

"Yaaaaaa," David said softly.

"You want to go to the pet store?

"Yaaaaa."

"I'm not sure what we could get him, but we can look." June thought about a turtle, or maybe a bird, but she wasn't sure how Mother would feel about it. Well, she'd cross that bridge when she came to it.

She wheeled David in the direction of the pet store, leaning far enough forward so that she could engage him in conversation. Inside the shop, they passed cages, perches, solariums, and desert habitats, and found their way into the aquarium aisle. David moved his legs in excitement. He made chirping and braying sounds.

"Well, I guess we're heading in the right direction," June said. "OK, you want to get him another fish for the aquarium? Let me know when you see what you want."

She pushed him past the variety of tanks, slowing in front of those she thought might be good companions for a goldfish. She paused in front of the one labeled "Black Molly."

David became more excited; it was evident he had found what he was looking for.

"It's not very pretty," said June. "You sure you don't want something brighter to add colour to the tank?"

David continued to make noises, and move his legs up and down in approval inside the straps.

"You're such a good brother. All right, I guess it's this one, but I'm not sure why." She looked around for a clerk to help her bag the shiny, black fish.

David made his *Star Wars* Chewbacca-like sound, and followed it with pops and whistles not unlike R2D2. June obviously was missing his attempt at drawing her attention to the *Star Wars* film. Still, his brother would be pleased.

Chapter 5
Treading Water

~~~~~~~~

A few weeks had passed since they had moved into their new home. Mother pulled a mass of mail out of the scratched metal mailbox that hung outside the front door. In the living room, Luke and David played while the TV sounded in the background. David's large wooden tray protruded from the front of his chair, and Luke had piled a tangled variety of dinosaurs onto it. He pulled one free and held the figure up, telling David the name of the fierce creature and imitating its sound. Luke was an "ex-spurt" on dinosaurs: he had seen *Jurassic Park* a hundred times.

There was lots of gnashing and crashing and yelping as the drama played out. David watched the scene in awe, imitating sounds more dinosaur-like than Luke's, especially the raptor's whistling and barking. Luke was impressed, but distracted by the stiff movement of Mother as she brushed passed him, separating the mail in an impatient manner. She slapped a stack of bills onto the kitchen table. Then she tore open a manila envelope, one of many Luke had seen before, and scanned the contents with an exasperated sigh.

"Luke, can you set up David's feed for breakfast?" she asked. "He gets one can for now. I'll give him his meds in a minute." Her voice quivered with emotion.

"What's in that?" he asked, pointing to the large envelope he assumed was responsible for her expression.

She leafed through a ten-page document before replying. "Another application that I don't have time to fill out for a program that will only put him on a waiting list."

She tossed the document on top of an overflowing pile of similar forms spilling out of a basket. Then she put her hands over her eyes, and Luke wondered if she was playing a game. But when she removed her hands from her face, her eyes were wet and slightly pink. "I think I'm in over my head," she said out loud to no one in particular. "I feel like I'm treading water with no land in sight." She sniffed in a breath of air, then went to the kitchen counter to pour David's meds and draw up the solutions in a variety of plastic syringes.

Luke always watched in fascination as she crushed pills and mixed them with water, drew up liquids, and lined up the syringes in a rainbow file. There was one of each: red, orange, yellow, white, cream, clear, and amber. These were paramount in his brother's ability to breath, digest, control pain, and sleep. They carried more weight for his survival than anyone knew.

Luke went to a box in the back closet, pulled out a can of formula, shook it hard, and lifted the pop-top with a snap. He returned to the living room, and stood on a chair close to David's IV pole, now next to him. The homemade feeding funnel was already in place at the top of the pole. Luke emptied the formula can into it, and watched as the contents drained into the metal spout and coursed down the plastic tube at a steady rate. He waited until the liquid dripped from the end of the long tube, then clamped it off. Then he secured the tip of the tube into David's "button," a small plastic device that had been medically inserted into his stomach. It had a short tube that extended into his gut. The outside part was flush with his skin. A port allowed the feeding tube to lock securely into place. The bond created an open flow-way into his belly, and caused him no discomfort or distress. The long feeding tube also had a chamber halfway down that adjusted the drip so that only so much at a time would go into David's stomach, a way to control the volume.

Luke unclamped the tube, and watched the flow pour into the chamber. By adjusting the roll-clamp, he slowed the drip down so it followed a counting pattern of "one one-thousand, two one-thousand" in his head.

Mother came in with the meds, and piled them onto David's lap. Her only response to Luke's help was to ask if he had made sure to get rid of air bubbles in the feed line to prevent discomfort.

She shut off the feed with the clamp, and undid the tube from the port. One at a time, the fluids were pushed through the button into David's stomach. She flushed them with a syringe of water, hooked the tubing back up, and restarted the feed by undoing the clamp. Then she slid the heavy tray back over the arms of the chair and secured it into place.

"How 'bout you boys sort socks before our appointment?" Mother turned up the volume on the TV to hear the news before going back into the kitchen.

"OK," Luke said. It was the better answer.

Grabbing a handful of socks, he tossed them onto the tray, then held up two. "Let's play Family Feeeooood, David Poole!" Luke said, mimicking the game-show announcer.

David wiggled happily in his chair and made his Chewbacca sound.

"Are these two socks the same?" Luke asked.

David glanced at both socks, and then produced a big smile.

"Survey says...*ding!* Fast work, David. Now you go to round two!"

Luke folded the socks and placed them back into the basket. He held up two coloured socks, and saw all expression leave David's face.

"Are these two socks red?" Luke waited to see if David would respond, but he remained motionless, his eyes locked on his brother. "Survey says...*ding!* Good job! Are they...blue?"

David didn't move.

"Are they yellow? Are they green?"

Luke watched his brother's expression transform into a broad smile. David kicked his feet inside the straps holding them in place on the foot pedals.

"Good work, Mr. Poole! *Ding, ding, ding!* The socks are green! Let's move on to round three." He folded the socks into themselves and placed them on the pile.

Then the phone rang, and Luke ran to grab it off the coffee table.

"Who you calling a nerd, nerd?" he said with a laugh.

"Who are you talking to?" Mother called from the kitchen.

"It's Sean, from my old school!"

Sean was the same age as Luke, and had lived next door. His family was originally from Ireland.

"Wassssup?" Luke asked. He listened for a moment, then called to Mother. "Sean wants to know if he can come over for a play date next week."

"Ah...well...I'm not sure. Tell him you'll call him back later and let him know. I don't know what's happening with work."

Luke turned back to the phone. "Mom says we'll have to wait and see. I can't wait to play you at video games again. I don't like playing with Jesse anymore. He's such an asshole. Yep, major asshole. He gets all crazy if he doesn't win. I'll call you again in a couple of days. *Ciao!*"

Mother came back into the living room, and started folding laundry in her lap. "Luke, did I hear you swearing?" she asked.

"No," Luke said quickly. He averted his eyes, while thinking about the choice word he used when he thought no one but David could hear.

Mother looked at David, whose face remained still. If someone was going to get into trouble, he wanted no part of it.

She glanced at Luke again, with a puzzled look on her face, but returned to her laundry as the boys continued sorting socks, two of which now hung off of Luke's ears, making her laugh along with David.

Then she leaned toward the TV, a stack of laundry neatly folded in her lap. "Shhh!" she said. As she reached for another garment, a reporter announced that the restructuring of city hospitals would continue, and positions would be held by those with seniority. More health-care workers would be put out of jobs.

Mother sat perfectly still; Luke wasn't sure she was breathing. He held up two socks and in a quiet voice said to David, "Survey says..."

But David's eyes were fixed on Mother.

The garment lay unfolded in her lap. "Things may be a little tough for a while," she said, "but we'll be fine." She tried to project calm, but her voice shook.

"What's wrong?" asked Luke, feeling uncertain about what to do.

She looked at the stack of applications for services, and grew weary at the thought of filling out more forms, which typically came back rejected because David was either too disabled or not disabled enough. It was known as hoop jumping, an exhausting and demoralizing exercise.

"Can't granny or uncle help?" Luke asked.

"I doubt it," she said sadly.

"We have some money from our birthday," he said. Miraculously, David and Luke's birthdays were both on October 21st but they were a year apart in age. Luke often tried to fool people into thinking they were twins.

She forced a smile. "Birthday money is not enough, sweetheart."

David made a series of sounds like cooing, much like a mother trying to sooth her distressed child.

"Mummmm," he said in a clear, soft voice.

The unexpected shock of the sound made her sit back. "Did he just say Mom?"

"I think so," Luke said.

Without warning, she began to bawl. The boys exchanged confused glances; Luke shrugged his shoulders and raised his eyebrows. He didn't understand the impact of his brother calling their mother Mom for the first time in ten years.

Mother quickly regained her composure. "We're going to be late for David's appointment," she said, wiping tears from her face.

The weekly appointment this time was with a specialist they had been waiting to see for several months. Getting organized always took a while.

She took David into the bedroom to change him and check for pressure spots. It was Luke's job to get the backpack and supplies ready. He walked past the fish tank, and pushed Bronte, the calico cat, off the edge of the table: Bronte appeared intrigued by the fish moving back and forth through the water.

The tank also held the latest family addition, the Black Molly he had received for his birthday the day before. He was thrilled to get it. Mother had gotten him a second-hand video game, although not the one he wanted. But David had given him something special; something wicked and cool. He stopped to watch the dark fish dart through the jungle of weeds and slide past Princess Leia. To no one's surprise, he had named it Darth Vader.

He watched it circle around the frilly pink Leia. *I wonder if a molly will eat a goldfish?* "One can only hope," he said aloud, with an evil grin.

Mother corralled the boys outside, loaded them into the van, and headed for the doctor's office. She checked the time and stepped on the gas. Smog thundered down the road.

David's mind was dreaming, soothed to sleep almost instantly by the rocking motion of the van.

At the same time, Luke's head was filled with a daydream of a pink ladyfish begging for mercy from a black-cloaked villain breathing heavily through a grilled mask.

Chapter 6
Swearing

Once they arrived at the hospital, Mother searched for a parking spot, always a chore. Because Smog exceeded the height limit, she couldn't use the parkade. Because the wheelchair lift opened from the side of the van, she couldn't park between vehicles. Because the handicapped parking stalls were not wide enough to allow her to push the chair off the lift between cars, she couldn't use most of them, either. There was only one place in the entire parking lot she could use easily, but someone was in it, so she dropped the boys off at the front of the hospital and searched for a spot on her own. *Thank goodness for Luke*, she thought. Without him, she would have had to leave David in the charge of a stranger until she could come back for him.

When she returned, Luke was racing David's wheelchair up and down the sidewalk. David's head was pressed against the headrest, his mouth wide open and his face filled with joy. He loved to go fast, and there was nobody better at racing him around than his brother.

Two women walking past the boys shook their heads in pity. "Those poor dears," one said. "What a life they must have."

Luke screeched to a stop and spun David around, pretending to be a racecar cutting a quick turn. He made screeching noises, much to

David's delight, until both boys collapsed against one another, laughing loudly. They didn't see the women staring at them, and the women didn't really see them, either.

Mother ignored the onlookers; she hurried the boys inside the building and headed for the elevator. They had waited months for this appointment and were going to be late because of parking. Her burning annoyance was beginning to crackle.

They arrived at the neurology department, and sat in the waiting room for nearly an hour before being called. Because this was a teaching facility, it was common to be seen by a resident physician before seeing the specialist, and today was no exception.

The trio was called into the examining room and, after more waiting, a tall young man wearing a white lab coat entered the room. He pulled up a chair in front of Mother and kept his eyes on the chart in front of him, flipping pages back and forth, searching for information.

"What brings you in today?" he asked, looking up at Mother with a friendly smile. He was clean-shaven and smelled of a spicy aftershave. His light brown hair was cut short and neatly arranged; he had difficulty meeting Mother's eyes.

"I'm here for David," she said, patting her son's knee. David responded by smiling at the doctor.

The physician briefly glanced at him, then returned to flipping chart pages. "And what can I do for you?" he asked, continuing to read.

"It's not for me, it's for my son," she said, patting David's leg again.

"Ah, and what's his problem?" the doctor asked, eyes fixed on the chart.

The boys exchanged glances. Luke recognized that the doctor was not comfortable with his sibling. He distracted David by slumping down in the chair, hanging his head over one shoulder, and allowing his tongue to hang out of his mouth.

Mother didn't notice, and continued the conversation. "David was referred to Dr. Pratt for a neurological assessment because he doesn't sleep without drugs. The medication he's presently on makes him drowsy in the morning, and we were wondering—"

The doctor interrupted her. "What's he on?"

"Chloral hydrate—10 cc per 100 ml." Mother tried to ignore his not yet having acknowledged her son. His attitude was not common from a medical professional, but neither was it unusual. At best, it was distressing and hurtful.

"We can certainly look at alternatives," the doctor said, finally turning toward David, who had picked up on the fun Luke started. Mimicking his brother, he cocked his head to one side, and his tongue hung out of his mouth. He closed his eyes for additional effect.

"Oh, my!" the doctor gasped. "You know, you don't have to do this. There are facilities for kids like him."

Mother sat stunned and silent.

"Look," he said, taking her hands. "I know it's hard, but you have another son to raise." He glanced toward Luke, who now sat upright. "According to my notes, you're a single mother. You're attractive, and you have one normal child who can amount to something. There are institutions for kids like him, and he'll never be anything but a burden to you." As he spoke, he gestured toward David with his head. "I know of other parents in your situation who were thankful for my advice and put their misfortunate child in a proper facility."

Luke sat forward in an effort to be part of the conversation, waiting for Mother to karate-chop the doctor, or yell in his face, or do *something*, but she remained quiet. She had heard it all before, and it always bewildered her. Finally, she spoke.

"First of all, at this time, there are no institutions here for 'kids like him,'" her fingers carved air quotes around the doctor's words, "unless I abandon him. Second, he's my son, and I love him, and I want to handle it—which I could, if only I could get the help I need without all the runaround. He may not meet your expectations, Doctor, but he meets mine."

"So forget the institutions," the doctor said. "There are good foster homes, you know, with caring parents who like to look after kids like him."

Kids like him. Mother cringed at the phrase; hearing it again made it even more offensive. What made him think strangers would love David or care for him better than she could? She didn't feel strong enough to ask. Angry and insulted, she let tears fill her eyes. He talked about her son like he was disposable.

"Well, it's just something to think over," he said, smiling. "I'll let Dr. Pratt know you're here." He stood up and headed for the door.

As he reached for the handle, David began to stir inside his straps. The sound was soft but audible, and there was no mistaking its intention. It was as recognizable as hail on tin, the braying of a horse, the whistle of a train. He clearly enunciated "aaaaho" to the doctor's back. The resident turned and looked questioningly at Mother. "What did he say?"

Her face remained blank, except for a slight twitch at the corner of her mouth. "Nothing."

Luke burst out laughing, then slapped a hand over his mouth to control himself.

"Fine." The doctor smiled stiffly, and shut the door behind him.

Luke burst into full laughter, and turned to look at Mother, whose face was stern. Her eyes twinkled, but her lips were unsmiling. Luke sat back into his chair, not sure what to do or where to look. All he knew was that he was probably in trouble.

"Where did David learn that word?"

Luke shook his head. "I don't know."

"Did you teach him that?"

"No, no! I would never say swear words," he said, shrugging his shoulders and spreading out his hands.

"Then where did he get it?"

"I don't know—maybe at school? They swear a lot at school. Danny Brook swears all the time. Or Isabelle...yeah, Isabelle. You should hear what she says!"

Mother cut him off. "Luke, just because David can't speak doesn't mean he can't hear. You need to be careful what you say in front of him. Besides, I was kind of hoping that some of his first words would be...I don't know...'Hi Mom,' or, 'I love you,' or maybe, 'pass the salt,' but definitely not—" She mouthed the offending word.

Luke looked at the floor.

"Luke, I'd like you to go outside so I can talk to your brother. There's a water fountain down the hall. Go grab a drink. We'll talk more about this later."

Luke felt angry. What was the fuss about? It had turned out to be a useful word! He pulled himself out of the chair, and gave his brother a quick glance before heading out the door.

"If I ever hear you using that word, Luke, you're grounded for a week," Mother said behind him.

"OK!" he said. He looked back with a scowl, only to catch sight of Mother placing a kiss in the middle of his brother's forehead. "Good boy, David." The door clicked shut.

"What the —?" Luke muttered in frustration, then waited alone in the hallway.

Chapter 7
Swallowing

After the appointment, Mother placed the prescription for David's new sleeping drug in her purse. She moved side by side with the boys, pulling the chair as she grasped the armrest on one side while Luke guided it from the other, hanging onto David's hand. Walking abreast made it seem like David was part of the group, rather than being pushed out in front like a warning flag.

Luke felt the warmth of David's hand and drew Mother's attention to it.

She stopped and placed her hand on David's forehead. "I think something is brewing. He feels a bit warm." She moved her hands over his cheeks. If he had a temperature, it was minimal. "You feel OK, David?"

"Yah," he said with a smile.

"Oh, great," Luke said. "Does this mean we can't go swimming today?"

They always had their swimming gear in the van. Swimming was an activity both boys enjoyed on a regular basis. There were swim suits, towels, life jackets, water walkers, and goggles; everything a water-lover needed to swim at a pool or a local lake.

"No, not today," Mother said, placing a hand on the top of David's head. "Besides, I think we should take this little beast o' burden for an ice cream. What do you think, Luke? But first I need to grab some cash."

Luke jumped up and down. David laughed, and his green eyes sparkled against the smile that lit his face. They continued walking side by side. The wheelchair shook as it crossed the unevenness of the mosaic-tiled floor towards the ATM machine.

Mother checked the balance in her account. She was overdrawn. She transferred $20 from her Visa account into her checking account. It wasn't the smart thing to do, but it was the only thing she *could* do. She realized that if her shifts became scarcer, this practice could become dangerous.

They walked over to the ice-cream counter, just outside the cafeteria. There were tables close by, with attached chairs in groups of four. Off to one side was a wooden bench with an ornate metal frame. A large, leafy tree stood on one side of the bench. It was rooted below the flooring and encouraged to grow under the skylight that ran the course of the ceiling. Mother and Luke sat down on the bench and pulled David up beside them.

Mother purchased two small Cokes and one small ice cream cone, heavily laden with a large scoop of chocolate. Handing the cone to Luke, she took a sip of the pop, then scooped a small sample of his ice-cream onto her finger, tracing it along the top of David's lip. He licked at it with his tongue, his face glowing with delight.

"It's good, eh, David? Want a little drink?" Luke asked. He sucked up a few drops of his pop into the straw then covered the end with his finger. Placing the straw over David's open mouth, not unlike a mother bird feeding her offspring, he slowly released his thumb, allowing the drop of fluid to fall onto David's tongue. David sucked on the solution in his mouth and shivered, his eyes rocking in his head from the sharpness of the taste and the fizz of the carbonate. His face bloomed into a smile as he swallowed. "Yummy, David?"

David had trouble coordinating breathing and swallowing, so the majority of his nutrition was absorbed by means of the tube in his stomach. If he took in a breath while swallowing, he would aspirate, inhaling food or liquid into his lungs, resulting in a coughing fit. An aspiration could turn into pneumonia, which meant hospitalization, and antibiotics for weeks or even months. Tasting was risky, but sometimes it was important to just be a kid, and Mother allowed a few risks from time to time.

"Can I give him another one?" Luke asked.

"No, I think that's enough for now." Mother put another dab of ice cream on David's lip. His eyes brightened and he made cooing noises as he licked the concoction off his mouth.

Luke was making fast work of his ice cream; some had dripped onto his arm and was meandering down toward his elbow. He slid his tongue along the course of the ice cream river to clean it off, and reappeared with traces of a chocolate beard attached to his chin.

David screeched with laughter.

Luke wiped the cold goo off of his face. "You think that's funny?" he asked jokingly, holding the ice cream up to David's nose. "Let's see how funny you think *this* is!"

David watched the ice-cream moving closer to his face. He let out a high-pitched shriek in anticipation of what was coming, and awkwardly attempted to block the onslaught with his hands.

"Stop it, you two!" Mother said in a distracted manner. Her attention was concentrated on a man in a white lab coat walking toward them. She waved her hand. "Hi, Tom!"

Luke recognized Tom as the head of the hospital orthopedic department where Mother worked as a nurse. He was a pleasant and kind man who had chatted with Luke a few times and often had gum in his pocket. He nodded to both boys, but provided only a weak smile for Mother. Luke was disappointed at not being offered any gum.

"Now is probably not the best time," Tom said, "but since you're here, can I talk with you a minute?"

"Certainly," Mother said. She looked at her sons. "Mind David," she said to Luke. She reluctantly followed Tom to the entrance of the cafeteria, several feet away.

Luke had lost interest in teasing his brother. He carefully doled out another drop of Coke, and David flinched and wiggled like a baby sucking on a slice of lemon.

Mother returned to the bench within a few minutes. She sat down beside the boys and tried to hold her voice steady. "He said that I'm about to be bumped from my job. That...that...bloody asshole!" she muttered angrily under her breath. She knew it had nothing to do with Tom.

David and Luke raised their eyebrows simultaneously as they looked at one another. Luke pointed an accusing finger at Mother's language, but said nothing out loud.

"It's probably going to be a while before we go swimming or to a movie, or do anything else, for that matter." Mother turned her head away and busied herself by sucking up the last of the pop through the straw. Tears dropped down onto her face, but she ignored them.

The boys watched her in silence, listening to her sniffles and the annoying sound of air being sucked through a straw in desperate search of something that was no longer there.

Luke lost his appetite. Why did this always happen to him? He took what remained of his ice cream and unceremoniously dropped it into the garbage bin. Then he sat back on the bench in a huff, consumed with self-pity.

Chapter 8
Bullying

~~~~~~~~

Nearly two months had gone by since the move, and the boys were settled into their new school. It was the first time they had attended the same place; David was usually in a different building, segregated from mainstream students.

In Luke's classroom, a ledge under a bank of windows held a variety of wire baskets, extending from one end of the shelf to the other, filled with papers, books, glue, scissors, and pencils. There were also a few plants in terracotta pots, which enjoyed the light coming from the large windows. A small cage housing a rose-hair tarantula rested on one corner of the shelf, where there was shade. Luke watched the spider slowly move its thick legs over the branch inside its habitat, then stop beside a plastic leaf as though it provided camouflage.

The bell rang for recess, and the rest of the students noisily headed for their backpacks to get a snack before going outside. His teacher, Ms. Wong, a tall, young Asian woman with long black hair, stood by her desk. She was flanked by several students, all of whom needed something: a Band-Aid, a pencil, a Kleenex, a snack, or a hug. Luke remained at his desk, observing the spider and feeling glum. He wasn't sure why he felt down; he just knew things were not right at home and he didn't like it.

Hektor, the class bully, stood next to a boy named Vincent. Hektor started moving in Luke's direction, deliberately bumping into his desk.

Luke looked up and felt his face tighten into a frown.

"What's the problem, Poole? Forget to wear your panties today?"

Luke looked at the round, insolent boy. Hektor was someone he avoided, since he was often angry, regularly disrupted the class, and seldom laughed at anything except other people's pain. He was more annoying than threatening, but Luke tried to ignore him as much as possible. He was learning that he needed to use his smarts to get the better of Hektor, who seldom used his own.

"Nope, I remembered my panties, but I think you forgot your manners. Leave me alone, Hektor. I'm not feeling well."

Hektor hated it when Luke didn't react to his taunting. But he thought he might have discovered a weakness, and how to get a reaction from the boy who seldom gave him the satisfaction of getting angry. "What's wrong, Poole? You gonna cry 'cause you got a moron for a brother?"

Luke snapped like a dried tree branch forced down across a knee. He jumped up and slammed his fist into Hektor's chest. The punch was a shock, and Hektor staggered backwards. Luke knocked him to the floor, and repeatedly smashed his fist against the boy's chest.

He felt a slim, strong arm slip under his belly, and the sensation of being pulled away from the wailing boy beneath him. Ms. Wong stood him on his feet, her arms still wrapped tightly around him.

"Sit over there, Luke," she said sternly, gently pushing him toward the desk behind her. She bent over the crying Hektor to check for damage. Satisfied he would survive, she stood the two boys together, but stayed between them in a crouched position.

Bystander Vincent told Ms. Wong he had seen everything. He looked in Luke's direction and gave the thumbs-up sign.

Luke nodded in appreciation.

Ms. Wong suggested that Vincent go outside, but he went in the opposite direction, towards the office. She turned to Hektor. "What happened?" she asked calmly, her arms folded and a look of concern on her face.

Hektor continued sniffling. "He hit me!"

"He started it," Luke interjected in self-defense.

"Not your turn yet." She looked back at Hektor. "Why did he hit you?"

"I don't know," he whined. "I was just walking by his desk and he attacked me!"

"You liar!"

Ms. Wong gave him a warning glance to stay quiet, then turned to the other boy again. "What you are saying, Hektor, is that you walked past Luke's desk, and he jumped up for no good reason and hit you? You never said anything or did anything?"

"No, I didn't do nuthin'."

"Hmmm," said Ms. Wong. "I don't think you're telling me everything, Hektor. Luke, tell me your side."

"He was bugging me."

"Go on," she said.

"And then he made fun of my brother."

She nodded slowly. "I see. OK, the two of you will escort me to the principal's office. I would say that both of you were in the wrong. We'll see what the principal says, but chances are you'll both receive detention and a call to your homes. Let's go, boys."

Hektor stepped back. "That's not fair! I didn't do anything!"

Luke groaned. The detention part was fine, but the call home was the last thing he needed. It would mean fewer privileges than he already had, and they were already at an all-time low.

He sensed the principal's disappointment when they entered his office. "These two boys were fighting in class," Ms. Wong said, with a protective arm around Luke.

"So I heard," the principal replied quietly. "I'll take it from here."

Following the conversation between the principal and Hektor, Luke had his one-on-one to decide his fate. He had apologized to Hektor for hitting him, he had accepted Hektor's attempt at an apology for his inappropriate behavior, and now sat waiting for the verdict from his mother. The principal put down the phone and looked at him. "She's not very happy about this," he said. "You will be spending the afternoon in Mrs. Gordon's class because you are on an in-school suspension for fighting."

Mrs. Gordon taught a Grade 6 class, and he felt intimidated by the older kids. He didn't want to go there. "I want to go home," he said.

"That's not an option, Luke," Mr. Becker said. His voice sounded soft and understanding. "Please go back to your classroom. Ms. Wong will have your stuff ready to go to Mrs. Gordon's class. I can understand how you feel, Luke. But fighting's not the solution."

"I know," Luke said wearily. He excused himself from the office, and slowly walked to his class.

Everyone was working quietly at their desks. Hektor sat at the back of the room on his own, cutting a mitten with scissors and littering wool fragments onto the floor. He ignored Luke's return.

Ms. Wong set the phone down into its cradle. "I'd like you to pack up your stuff. That was your mom on the phone. She's coming to get you."

Luke's feelings soared. He was going home! How perfect was that? Even if he might be banished to his room, at least he wouldn't be in a classroom with a bunch of Grade 6 kids he didn't know. His mother had come to his rescue. She must have known it wasn't his fault and that he was simply defending his brother. Finally, she was on his side!

He was pulling his arms through the straps of his backpack when Ms. Wong came to help him straighten the straps on his shoulders. "Your detention will begin tomorrow instead. Right now, head down to your brother's classroom so you can meet your mother there. She has to take David to the doctor. He's sick."

Luke's spirits deflated like air hissing out of a balloon. This wasn't about him at all. It was about David, and the fact that Mother did not want to come back to get him later. He was just tagging along to David's doctor's appointment.

He shuffled his feet as he exited the classroom, feeling annoyed, disappointed, and sorry for himself. Besides, he still had a detention and all the fuss, as usual, was about David.

Chapter 9
Sulking

Luke pushed open the door into the doctor's office on the second floor of the Tower Building, followed by David and Mother. The room was crowded with children in wheelchairs and babies in strollers, curving around a large fish tank in the middle of the floor. Brightly coloured fish floated around the rocks and corral, creating a lively display. Various types of anemone adorned the rock formations, and small starfish, relaxed and content, were splayed lazily against the "reef."

Luke thought it odd that one of the mothers also had a small animal kennel at her feet, which housed a fluffy grey cat. There were rumours that Dr. Liam used to be a veterinarian, so some people brought their sick animals along with their children for the visit. Despite the enormous aquarium, the cat seemed pleased to lie in the bottom of its carrier and snooze.

Luke pulled out toys from one of the drawers beneath a bench seat against the wall. Many of the children sat in their parent's laps to make more room in the crowded space. Every available place to sit was taken, so Mother had to stand with David next to the fish tank. He loved to watch the fish. The water and the flowing movement of the beautiful creatures had a calming effect on him.

Mother approached the counter to speak to Wanda, the receptionist, busy on the phone while other lines rang. She caught Mother's eye and acknowledged her presence with a wink. Three clinic nurses floated behind the reception area, occupying themselves with charts and paperwork.

Wanda put the next call on hold and addressed Mother. "You made it!" she said as another line began to ring.

"Thanks so much for getting us in on such short notice," Mother said. "The nurse at the school called me and said he had a temperature of 41 degrees and that his breathing was raspy."

"You know you can call us anytime and we'll fit him in." The packed waiting room was proof she was not the only parent of a severely compromised child with that privilege. "You might have to wait a bit, though. I'll have to squeeze you in between appointments."

"Not a problem. We're glad to just be here." Mother went back to stand next to David, while Wanda returned to her calls.

After an hour, and a few stories read aloud, they were led into an examining room. Mother positioned David's chair in the small space next to the examining table, and sat in a chair by the sink. Luke sat cross-legged on the floor beside David. Behind him, a collage of pictures, showing many of Dr. Liam's young patients, covered the wall. These picture murals were proudly displayed in each of the six examining rooms. Luke often looked to see if he could find a photo of himself and his brother, but not today. Today he was sulking. He had a plastic airplane in his hand, but made no attempt to make it fly.

David quietly watched him. The nurse came into the room to examine David and gather information. She was thorough and kind, and looked into his eyes when she asked the questions, which Mother answered for him. He beamed at her as she stroked his cheek and took his temperature. He batted his long lashes flirtatiously, and made a series of cooing sounds and attempts at speech. When the examination was done, the nurse placed the chart in the plastic holder on the door in preparation for Dr. Liam and, much to David's disappointment, left the room. All the nurses were pretty, and he never missed an opportunity to interact with them.

His head swung up when he heard the familiar tune being whistled in the hall. He didn't know the song, but it was always the same tune. He kept his eyes on the door, waiting for it to open.

Dr. Liam strode into the room, wearing a beige-striped shirt with white collar and cuffs. He wore a colourful, Spiderman-in-action tie. Spider webs jutted out from the superhero's wrists as he leapt for a skyscraper.

"How are you, Poole?" Dr. Liam asked Mother. He tossed the chart onto the counter and washed his hands at the sink.

"I'll be better when you tell me what's going on with David."

"The notes say our boy has a temperature." Dr. Liam moved toward David, and bent to ruffle Luke's hair before addressing his patient. "Hello, Dawwwvid. You sick?" He put his hands on both armrests of the wheelchair and leaned into David, touching foreheads. David smiled.

Dr. Liam could feel the heat coming from his patient's skin, and he could hear David's raspy breathing as his chest rose and lowered.

"The school nurse said he had a temperature of 41 degrees. His breathing has been labored, and there's a bit of a wheeze to it," Mother said.

Dr. Liam nodded. "You don't sound so good, David." He pulled a small scope from the wall and peered into David's ears to check for redness or fluid. "Open up, buddy." He positioned the light to look down David's throat for any signs of redness or inflammation. Then he slipped his stethoscope from his neck and placed the plugs in his ears, lowering his head as he put the disc against David's chest.

"It's his upper airway," he said after a moment, slinging the stethoscope back around his neck. "It's not too bad right now. Just give him Ventolin and chest physio and see how he does. You got anything for his fever?"

"Yes, and I also have a form from the school nurse. She wants to know the medical condition of his chest." She unfolded the paper and handed it to him.

"I don't know what they want me to say. He has cerebral palsy as the result of a premature birth at twenty-four weeks gestation, and his lungs have been compromised. 'What is the condition of the said patient's lungs'?" he read. He scribbled his response. "Crrraaappy!"

He signed the form and handed it back to Mother. "You can fill out his name and stuff."

"Crappy?" she repeated. "Is that it?"

He placed both hands over Luke's ears and whispered to her. "Well, I could have said effin' crappy, which is closer to the truth, but I didn't think they'd like that on their fancy form."

Mother laughed. "Don't worry, something tells me Luke's probably heard that word before."

Luke gave his mother an exasperated look.

Dr. Liam moved toward the sink to wash his hands again. "We've been watching this boy for eleven years and no matter how sick he gets, he doesn't give in. So far, he has been hospitalized, what...," he glanced at the front of the chart, "...twenty-five times, and he continues to baffle the medical community and beat the odds. Kids like David have a resiliency that is second to none. All we can do is address the symptoms and keep a close watch over him. The rest is up to him—and Him," he said, pointing to the sky.

Mother nodded, but the look of concern remained on her face.

Dr. Liam held out his arms for a hug. "I think you need one of these," he said as Mother rose to receive his warm embrace.

Then he released her and turned his attention to the younger brother. "And what about Luke? How's this young buck doing?"

"Fine," Luke mumbled. "Just peachy."

"You don't sound peachy to me." Dr. Liam leaned on David's chair and whispered, "I think you should take your brother to the arcade for a few games. He's a bit cranky."

Luke's eyes brightened at the notion of going somewhere with lots of excitement and crazy sounds. He looked at Mother to check for approval, but didn't see any. Then he remembered the fighting at school.

As Dr. Liam reached the door, Mother asked after his wife. "How's the missus doing?"

"Oh, she's great. She's got herself involved in some cause to rescue stray dogs or something."

"How are the kids?"

"Good. You'd think someone with five kids wouldn't have time to be involved in all this other stuff, but she seems to pull it off. She's quite amazing...keep me in the loop about how your boy's doing." He turned and walked through the open door.

Luke watched as the doctor scooped up a small child who ran toward him. The youngster giggled as he carried her toward a different examining room, her tiny fingers wound up in his hair. The child's mother followed them into the room and the door shut behind them, muffling the sound of Dr. Liam's familiar whistle.

Luke dragged himself up from the floor and waited for Mother to pull open the door. "We should get David home to bed," she said. "I don't want this to get any worse."

He pushed David toward the doorway. "Sometimes I don't think you care about me. We never do things for me. I'm not important at all."

"Don't be silly, Luke. What would I do without you? Please take David out and wait in the hall. I have to go to the front desk." She slid past the boys to talk to Wanda about another appointment.

Sure, I'm important. I'm important because someone has to look after David.

In spite of his foul mood and feeling undervalued, as soon as he was in the hall alone with David, his annoyance lifted and his capacity for adventure returned. "Hey, I wonder if we could get around the hallways and back here before Mom comes out! Ready? Let's go!"

David shrieked with delight, and they were off, running down the hallway, taking the sharp corners at full speed in an effort to get back to the door before Mother emerged. They laughed as they made their mad dash like a runaway train. Through the course of the run, David's lethargy disappeared, and Luke's distress vanished. But the moment Mother appeared, he only heard her rebuke. "Luke! You're going to make him sicker. Stop!"

He felt the bite of her gruff words, and the sting of tears in his eyes.

Chapter 10
Trick-or-Treating

Luke loved October. It meant both birthday and Halloween celebrations. This year, though, their birthdays had remained low key. They had hot dogs, which were always good, and a cake. There were few presents, but he had to admit his Darth Vader fish from David was pretty special.

He had wanted to get David a toy, but all the ones they saw at the big toy department store were not within David's physical limitations, let alone Luke's own price range. As an alternative, Mother took Luke to the pet store, Let's Paws, to find something. David had difficulty with both gross and fine motor movements, making it next to impossible for him to hold things. But pet stores offered chew toys that were often softer and easier to manipulate, not to mention less expensive.

Luke found two options: a brightly coloured ball with a bell inside, and a grey rubber mouse that squeaked when squeezed. He chose the mouse; it was cool, and he could torment David with it. As it turned out, David loved the mouse and it fit easily into his hand. Bronte and Montgomery eyed it as well.

At first Luke wasn't excited about Halloween, since he knew they wouldn't be buying costumes this year. But he was pleased when they made a trip to the thrift store to buy items to create costumes instead. David agreed to be a pirate, and Luke wanted to be a vampire.

On All Hallows' Eve, Mother worked an eleven-hour shift at the hospital in the ER. As warned, she had been bumped from her position in orthopedics, and was now grabbing shifts that came open in other departments, which were few and far between. Auntie June had agreed to take the boys door to door to show off their costumes and collect a few treats.

It was the end of October, and there was a skiff of snow on the ground, as well as a chill in the air. Luke put on warm clothes under his costume and got ready to go. His excitement was high, and he felt thrilled about all the candy he would receive.

Auntie June and her husband, Rayne, had arrived slightly later than intended following a medical appointment. Rayne Littlechild was a big man in his late thirties, over six feet tall, with warm-brown skin. His black hair hung almost to his waist, and was often pulled back into a tight braid. A carpenter by trade, he was, like June, of Cree heritage.

They had met on campus at the university when they were younger. His circumstances hadn't allowed him to complete his degree in behavioural sciences. Still, Rayne was more of a handyman than anything else, and so he had turned to fixing things. The boys often called him Ray and knew the amusing story behind his name. His mother had named him Dwayne, after a cherished uncle, but the nurse who recopied the baby's name couldn't properly make out his mother's writing. As a result, his birth certificate claimed him to be Rayne Michael Littlechild. He didn't mind his name and had never tried to change it. He joked that his middle name was Mann, in a nod to the late-1980s film *Rain Man*.

Rayne and June began getting things ready for the "little monsters" that would visit. There was a pumpkin with a candle inside it on display, and paper spiders the boys had made in school taped to the front window. The door was open to receive ghouls and goblins, and a big pot of individually wrapped suckers sat on the floor.

June felt miserable, but her sad demeanor remained unnoticed by the boys. Her husband strode up behind her and pulled her into a strong embrace. "It's OK," he said softly. "It just wasn't meant to be right now."

Her eyes burned with tears as she tried to shake off the disappointment once again. She and Rayne had been married for nearly ten years, and in all that time she had failed to become pregnant. She desperately wanted a child, and had gone through years of various treatments, but nothing seemed to work. Today was yet another confirmation that it wasn't going to happen for them. "Infertile," she had been called. "Undeserving" was what she tortured herself with in private moments.

"The Creator is just making sure you're ready for the right one," her husband said, turning her toward him. "June, there are many women who become mothers without effort, but you have longed, cried, and prayed for a child. When you're a mother, and I have no doubt you will be, you'll be prepared. In the meantime, your waiting has given you additional insight, compassion, and grace. Remember, my wife, you're not alone."

June melted into him and let the tears flow. After a moment, she collected herself and began getting things organized to take the boys on their walk. Regardless of her own sadness, she would not let it ruin their joy. Besides, being with the boys made her happy. They were a delight to be with despite their differences and challenges.

Standing close to David's chair, June felt his hand brush against her sleeve, jingling the tiny bells sewn into the seam. She always seemed to have bells sewn into various garments, whether a skirt, a blouse, or a scarf. As David pulled on her sleeve, Luke asked why she always had bells on her clothing.

"I'm sure I've told you the story before," she said. "Maybe we'll keep it for another time. Let's get ready to go." She wasn't in the mood for her own stories, even pleasant ones.

She drew up the hood of her coat to shield herself from the lightly falling snow. Luke was already at the door with his loot bag in hand. She pushed David's chair to the front door and out onto the sidewalk, giving her husband a quick kiss before maneuvering down the sidewalk with Luke hanging on to her hand. He skipped along, his black cape flapping behind him.

Rayne threw a wave from the doorway as he waited for trick-or-treaters to come calling. He knew how upset his wife felt after discovering the treatment had failed again. He would man the door and enjoy a treat or two while he waited—even if lollipops weren't his favourite thing.

As June and the boys reached the bottom stair of the first house, Luke ran to the door to ring the bell. He held out his bag when the neighbour answered, and she tossed a few candies into it. She looked past him to David and waved. "Where's your brother's bag?"

"Oh, he doesn't have one," replied Luke. David was unable to eat by mouth; there was no sense in getting him candy. Or was there?

"I'll give you some for him, too." She threw extra treats into the bag.

"Thank you!" Luke knew a good thing when he saw it and said nothing more. He turned and ran down the steps to June. "I'll race you to the next house!"

Before June and David had even reached the walkway, he had gotten the candy and run back down the stairs. The couple at the doorway waved as Luke dashed off to the next home. After several stops, his bag looked rather heavy.

"Maybe one more house and then we should start back," June said.

"No, no!" Luke said, pointing in a specific direction. "Mom said we could go all the way to the end of that street."

"I see that your neighbours are very generous with their treats. Your bag is very full."

He shrugged and started toward the next house, hoping to get there before June noticed what he was doing.

"Luke, are you asking for extra treats?"

He stopped short. "No."

"OK. Let me try that again. Are people offering you extra candy for David?"

He shifted the bag from one hand to another. "Maybe."

"I see," June said, trying to hide her smile. "Let's keep going, then."

Keeping within hearing distance, she listened to his conversations.

"My brother doesn't have his own bag, so you can put his stuff into mine," he said enthusiastically, and the occupant of the house gladly provided additional candy. "Oh, and he especially likes those!" he said at the last house, pointing to the small chocolate bars in the mix of candy in the bowl.

They turned back toward their own house after they had reached the end of the street. Both boys looked satisfied and happy with their neighbourhood jaunt.

June and Rayne helped the boys get undressed and into their pajamas before examining the spoils of their adventure. Luke was impressed with all the candy he had scored. He dumped the contents of his bag onto the floor like it was treasure from a deserted island, rubbing his hands together with glee. Then he began to sort it into piles of most desirable and least desirable.

"How are you going to share your candy?" June asked.

"What?"

"I think that half of it is David's, or least that's why you have so much."

Luke's brain went numb. What did she mean? "David can't eat candy," he said.

"Yes, but you got it for him, didn't you?"

Luke nodded his head, considering the question. "Yeaaah...I guess so."

"Then you need to share it with him."

"But he can't eat it!"

"Then he gets to decide who he will give his share to. How about Rayne? David, can Rayne have the candy Luke collected for you?"

David displayed a big smile.

Rayne didn't often get to eat junk, at least not without hearing about it. *This is working out rather well*, he thought.

"But that's not fair," Luke said, pouting. "I didn't get it for Ray!"

"I know, but you made people believe you were getting it for David, when you were actually getting it for yourself. What you did was wrong. It's like lying. You shouldn't use David's disability to get things for yourself."

"Fine!" He knew what she meant, but still struggled with the idea that he had carried all that extra candy for nothing.

June helped him sort it into two piles, and placed the second lot into a spare bag. Rayne picked up the bag and shuffled his hand inside, looking for a piece of toffee.

June squeezed the top of the bag and pulled it away from him.

"Isn't this mine?" Rayne asked.

"Hardly," she said, patting his stomach. "I know some kids who'd really appreciate this." Students at the elementary school where she was vice-principal would love the unexpected windfall.

She walked away clutching the bag, leaving Rayne with one piece of toffee, Luke with half his original loot, and David with a pirate patch still covering one of his brightly shining eyes.

Chapter 11
Saving

October dragged. Mother felt it took forever to pass, and that each moment blended into the next with no downtime. It wasn't that there were good days and bad days, but, instead, good minutes and bad weeks. Still, eventually time moved on, and so did the season.

The weather turned abruptly in November, changing the scenery from a blanket of leaves to a blanket of snow. Graders plowed down roads to reduce the risk of accidents and increase the chances of successfully getting to a destination. Snow did not fall gradually or gently; it fell in a massive dump, instantly transforming the landscape into a magical winter wonderland. Winter in Alberta usually dominated eight out of the twelve months of every year, allowing for what felt like one month of spring, one month of summer, and two months of fall. The snow-covered landscape was beautiful to look out onto from inside a warm home. Pushing through tons of snow was a different matter, particularly when steering a wheelchair.

Mother and Luke had finished yanking David's chair through the snowy parking lot to the side of the van. She had shoveled a path to the vehicle, but the narrow wheels snagged on bits of ice and patches of snow, which slowed or stopped their progress. The effort was tiring:

one pushed and the other pulled. Mother often parked out front by the sidewalk, but the increasing height of the grader rows blocked the sidewalk from the street. None of her complaints to government offices ever produced anything more than good intentions. She was obliged to use the spot behind their home, which was seldom cleared by the government-run housing development. Each time it became necessary, she asked herself why they still lived in this province. The answer was always the same: no money to go anywhere else, and no other pediatrician she trusted as much as Dr. Liam.

Once she had the boys safely strapped in, she manipulated the green beast out of the parking lot and headed north. School buses weren't running because of heavy snowfall. The boys would have to come along to her appointment with the district member of the legislative assembly (MLA) to discuss her job and the difficulties that came with being bumped to eleven-hour night shifts. She loved her work, but the hours created problems with care for her boys.

The sidewalk outside the government building had been cleared of snow to make their going easier. However, the wheelchair ramp to the front door had not been shoveled, slowing their progress. More than pushing, Luke made fine work of sliding on the ice and falling face first into the clean snow. David laughed at his brother. Mother sighed; they were going to be late.

At the top of the landing, a turnstile led into the building. Turnstile doorways were fairly common, since they decreased the amount of cold air that came in with every visitor during winter months. They also caused problems for many disabled people. It was impossible to get both David and her into the space to turn him around. Another door a few feet back and off from the ramp was locked.

They would be later than they already were.

"I need you to stay here with David, and don't do anything silly," Mother warned Luke. "I'll have to find someone to unlock the door."

"What do you mean, don't do anything silly? Why would you say that?"

"Because sometimes you do. If David didn't have a disability, I'm sure he'd be the one looking after you. Wait here at the top of the ramp."

Her words stung Luke. He watched her slip through the turnstile doorway. Why didn't she get it? Luke wondered. Why didn't she see his worth? If David was in danger, he would be the one who would save him. *If David was a little bit in danger and I saved him, then I would be the hero*, he thought.

That sounded good. He drummed his fingers across his cheek as he looked back at the ramp. There was an entrance into the building at the bottom, and on the other side of that the exit for vehicles. A "ping" sound to caution pedestrians accompanied each vehicle leaving the building.

Luke moved to the top of the ramp, gripped the railing, and slid a short way before running back up. He slid down a couple of feet further. This was fun!

David began kicking inside his straps, his body moving in excitement as he watched Luke.

"You want to go sliding, David? We could give it a little try," Luke said. After all, he could say the brakes gave way on the chair and he had to dive down the ramp to save his brother. Yes, that would be good. Show her.

He got behind David's chair and pulled off the brakes, moving him onto the top of the ramp. "Ah!" David said.

Luke held the chair steady as they started a slow glide down the ramp. The ping sounded, signaling a vehicle exit, but he was too busy to notice. The combined weight of David and the chair were more than he could handle, and they slid faster and faster down the ramp, their descent barely slowed by the snow. Luke hung on behind, trying to dig in his boots. A second ping warned them of another moving vehicle as they hit the bottom level of the ramp. Luke turned his body sideways, sliding along with the chair as they sped into the path of an oncoming car exiting the lot.

A delivery truck pulled up and stopped at the edge of the sidewalk, blocking their course into the exit lane. Luke lost his grip on the chair and had to let go, sprawling face down on the snow-covered sidewalk. David and his wheelchair slammed sideways into the truck. Securely strapped, David felt only a severe rocking. The appearance of a strip of dirt on the side of his snowsuit was all there was to show for the collision. But the impact had scared him and he began to cry.

The driver ran around to the side, having no idea what had hit his truck. It might well have been a moose, or a deer, and he was surprised to see two small boys, one in a wheelchair, the other raising himself up from the ground. He held out a hand to Luke and pulled him up. "What's going on?" he asked. An exit ping sounded again. "You two could have been seriously hurt or killed."

Luke looked back up at the ramp, fumbling for an answer. "I was trying to get my brother up the ramp, and I lost control of his chair," he said.

David bawled loudly. Luke tried to shush him, annoyed that his brother was being such a baby.

"Is he OK?" the driver asked.

"He's fine. It just scared him, is all."

David swung his arm out as far as he could to hit his brother, but missed.

"Where is your mother?"

"Oh...she's parking the van." Luke glanced at David's pouting face. They both knew he was lying.

The driver straightened David's muddied toque, and he appeared to calm down after his terrifying ride. "Your mother shouldn't be leaving you two out here by yourself. Maybe I should talk to her."

"No, no, no," Luke said. "You don't need to do that, but if you could help us get up the ramp, she should be back any minute."

The driver obliged, sliding occasionally on patches of ice hidden under the snow. When they reached the top, he locked David's brakes into place. "You sure you two are OK?" he asked, looking at David's face.

"We're fine, thanks," said Luke.

The driver headed toward his truck. "All right, but be careful!" His voice echoed through the parking lot.

Luke felt a light breeze at the back of his neck, then felt David's fist against his head.

"Ow, that hurt!" He looked back at David, scowling.

The side door opened and Mother emerged with a man holding a key.

"Sorry that took so long. Let's go, you guys," she said, moving toward David's chair.

Luke stood behind her, jacket zipped, hat in place, mittens on. David's jacket was twisted, his hat askew, and one mitten was missing. A strip of mud stretched from the top of his head and ran down the side of his body to the top of his boot.

"Should I even ask?" She glared at Luke. "I cannot trust you to watch over your brother for one minute without something happening. What's the matter with you?"

"Me? I was trying to save him! I was a hero!" Luke shouted in self-defense. "His chair went backwards down the ramp!"

"Really? And who took the brakes off at the top of the ramp?"

"I didn't do anything wrong."

"Luke, we're going to be late." Mother pushed David's chair and didn't turn as she spat out, "I need to see this man to ask for help. You and David will sit in the waiting room together. Please, please don't do anything impulsive!"

"What does that mean?" he asked.

"Don't do anything without thinking! Consider the consequences before you do something!"

Luke scowled, and followed her through the door labeled Government Offices. She was greeted by a woman who took her information and suggested the boys sit next to the terrarium so they could watch the reptiles.

Mother sat, looking around at the other people waiting, and felt a strained silence. The room felt dead. She was called within minutes to meet with the MLA for their district. Before leaving the waiting room, she turned to Luke and gave him a warning look. *Don't do anything foolish.*

Luke shook his head and turned away. *She has no faith in me at all.*

Chapter 12
Pleading

~~~~~~~~~~~~~~~

Before Mother entered the office, she looked back to see Luke tapping on the side of the terrarium on the table beside his chair. She was about to go back and caution him again, but saw there was a screened lid on the top of the container. "Don't tap on the glass," she said.

"Right," Luke said as she disappeared through the office door. He continued tapping.

The MLA came around from the side of his desk to greet her. He was a tall man with kind eyes, and walked with a bit of a limp. She suspected from the way he moved that he probably had a prosthetic leg. If his own physical condition was compromised, he might be more sympathetic to her plight.

"Glad to meet you, Mrs. Poole," he said. "How can I help?"

She sat on a wooden chair across from him and met his eyes. "Well," she began, "I have a problem. I'm a nurse at one of the hospitals, and they've been restructuring medical-staff positions. My previous job was in the hospital's outpatient orthopedic department, so I worked day shifts, with weekends off. But they've bumped me to a floating position, where I often work eleven-hour night shifts." She took a ragged breath as emotion seeped into her explanation. "I have two sons, ten and eleven years old, and I'm a single parent. My older son was born with a severe form of cerebral palsy due to a premature birth and needs medical care. The only thing David can do independently is smile. I can't let just anyone look after him because he's one of those kids who can be fine one minute and in a state of emergency the next. He requires expert attention, medical treatments, tube feeding, and lifting out of the wheelchair for naps and diaper changes." She sat further back and exhaled.

"What are you doing now for care?"

"Both boys go to a regular daycare for a few hours after school, and then I pick them up. I leave for work at nine o'clock and I don't get home until after nine in the morning. So the worker, who spends the night, has to get them off to school as well. It costs nearly $30 an hour for a nurse to look after David alone, which is more than what I make right now."

"Can't you get cheaper care?" the MLA asked, as he rummaged through papers on the edge of his desk.

"Yes, I could," she said, "but it may jeopardize David's safety—the average person doesn't have adequate medical training."

The MLA ignored the tension rising in her voice. "Parents of disabled children don't come with medical degrees, but they manage fine. Caregivers can be trained. I can tell you that the government will not pay for childcare for your sons over the period of time you need. The problem is the kind of work you do. The only reasonable thing I can suggest is for you to change your job."

She felt like she'd been slapped. "What I do is not a *job*. It's my career."

"We could probably help you with some of your daycare expenses that fit within the normal spectrum, but, unfortunately, that's all. You would have to change what you do for a living and get a job with regular hours. The shift work is your biggest problem here."

Mother covered her face with her hands. She felt her words choke themselves out of her mouth. "So I'm supposed to forget my training, work as a waitress, and try to raise two boys on the hopes of decent tips?"

The MLA tried to gently push aside the desperation in her response. "I'm sure that is not your only option. Besides, your boys must have a father. Is their dad not providing adequate support for them? I hate to say it, but this is more a matter of child support than government support."

"Their dad has gone missing."

"Missing or ran away?"

"We don't know. Either way, his contribution would have been minimal."

"Why do you say that?"

"Because whatever I would have received from him would have affected my living expenses as well as the cost contribution for David's medical supplies. The more income I have, the more they take away."

"He could have agreed to provide you additional assistance on the side."

"I doubt he would have done that."

"You must have some savings or RRSPs?"

"Not anymore. When I applied for government housing, I was told I couldn't have any savings or RRSPs in order to qualify. The house we were in wasn't in my name, so I had no claim to it either. The money that I did get went toward an overpriced wheelchair-accessible vehicle that we needed in order to accommodate David's chair."

"I see," the MLA responded politely. "In that case, all I can suggest is for you to find a good-paying job that has daytime hours with weekends off. That's the only advice I can offer you. If you have any other questions, please give my office a call and we'll see what else we can do." He smiled at her from across the table in a gesture of goodwill, but Mother felt her world collapsing. She raised her head, making eye contact with the man she had hoped would be on her side.

"Please," she whispered, "I'm begging you. I don't know what else to do. I'm drowning." Tears sprouted from her eyes.

"I'm sorry," he said. There is nothing more I can do to help you." He reached behind his chair and pulled a sheet of Kleenex out of a floral-printed box on the counter. In a last-ditch effort, he asked, "What about family? Can they help you?"

She shook her head. "No, they have their own circumstances. Besides, some of them believe the position I'm in is of my own doing. Others find it easier to turn a blind eye to what makes them uncomfortable. Some believe, however falsely, that families with disabled children are pretty much handed everything for free."

"Oh, my," the MLA said. He put the whole Kleenex box in front of her. The first tissue had dissolved into a clump of wetness from tears and mucous.

Mother pulled herself up. Her eyes searched his, but he looked away, avoiding the pain on her face. She heard confused, chaotic sounds from the other side of the door, but her raw bewilderment kept her from registering them. How would she tell her boys their situation had moved from bad to worse?

Tears flowed down her face again. Crying had become as common as breathing. She studied the MLA's eyes. "You know, I used to support this government, but every time I turn around, I wonder why. It seems they don't care about the people who struggle, just the deficit and making big business bigger."

The MLA offered a comforting smile. "The government never forced you into a professional choice—you made it yourself. Your circumstances have changed, so now you need to do some things to accommodate the change. I wish I could help you more, but I can't."

She sucked in air, got up, and walked out of a room filled with despair into a waiting room filled with commotion.

Oh, God. The shrill sound of Luke's young voice rose above the din of frantic adult voices. *What has he done now?*

Chapter 13
Investigating

~~~~

Luke had tried to make himself comfortable in a stiff leather chair. The table beside it held a glass tank containing three lizards. The first lizard was large with black-and-red markings, and bulging eyes. It crawled across a leafy branch poised in the centre of the tank. A second lizard, with dark-grey bumpy skin, tried to hide itself among the leaves attached to the branch. The last one, long and thin, lay across a rock in one corner, appearing undisturbed. A few browned pieces of neglected apple lay in the bottom of the terrarium.

Luke was fascinated by these creatures. He pulled David closer to see them. David was more interested in the other people in the waiting room, presenting bright smiles and chirping sounds to anyone passing by. But he was willing to go along with Luke and show interest in the reptiles, too.

"Look at these, David," Luke said. "They're like little dinosaurs! I learned about them in school. They're called reptiles and eat bugs and fruit. They have scaly skin and feel weird when you touch them. They aren't slimy, though."

The screened lid had turn locks to hold it in place. He undid the locks and pushed, moving it slightly. The receptionist glanced up and looked over her glasses. She grinned at Luke. "Everything OK?"

"Yes, fine," he replied. "What are the names of the lizards?"

She named them, tallying with her fingers. "The big one is R2D2, the grey one is Han Solo and the small one is—"

Luke hung his head. *Oh, no, here it comes.* Blasted Star Wars had polluted his life! *She's going to say...*

"—Yoda."

Thank God.

Luke slid himself out of the chair and crouched in front of the creatures. "I bet they're hungry. Look at that rotten apple in there," he said to David.

David was more interested in the woman sitting next to him. She wore a thick coat, with a trim of fur around the collar. It probably felt soft. Three men sitting opposite her all read newspapers, their eyes glued to the printed pages. One wore sloppy jeans, the pant legs jammed into open work boots. Another wore a hoodie, with a loosely tied drawstring at the neck. The last man sat in a wrinkled suit with his legs crossed, which raised his pant cuffs above his socks, each patterned differently from the other.

A white container under the table caught Luke's attention. Marked Lizard Food, it was the size of an ice-cream pail and had a snap-on lid.

Luke reached for it. "Hey, look at this! We could give them a few more bits of apple because the stuff in the tank looks bad. I can push the lid over and drop some in."

The receptionist glanced up at Luke from her desk. "Nooooo!" she yelled. But she was too late.

Chapter 14
Jumping

~~~~~~~~

Later, Luke wasn't sure how to describe the action in the container when he lifted the lid. It was like bubbles forcing their way to the top of a glass of Coke, breaking the surface in a mad rush. Or like popcorn, with its snapping sound, bursting up from the depths of the container to hit the lid and spill out onto the floor, bouncing in all directions. All he knew was that once he opened the lid to Pandora's Box, the situation was out of his control. Small, freedom-seeking crickets appeared everywhere. The room was alive with them.

Mother entered the short hallway leading into the waiting room and was met with the sight of people gamely diving into corners and running across the room, frenziedly grabbing minute green flying objects. The woman in the fur coat smacked feverishly at her collar, now a Velcro-like landing for high-jumping crickets. Yanking one off, she tossed it into the container, and the receptionist slammed the lid.

The man with the steel-toed boots walked gingerly across the carpet as he tried to scoop a few off the top of the counter. One tried to bury itself face down into the open top of his boot, while more surfaced from the other boot.

Luke, hiding behind the leather chair, grabbed one and placed it into the bucket.

Mother joined the group, seizing a few of the jumpers before they got away. She gave Luke 'the look', knowing she would find out details later and have to offer appropriate apologies for her son's behaviour.

David laughed, a wide, open-mouthed laugh, enjoying the sound and sight of everyone trying to take control of the chaos. A hopper hit him on the side of his cheek and dropped to the floor. He snapped his mouth shut, uncertain that he hadn't trapped the creature inside. He frantically moved his tongue around to be sure his mouth was empty, then kept his lips pressed together.

Other office workers had come into the waiting room to help retrieve the crickets and return them to the bucket. They were captured on the fax machine, photocopier, bookshelf, table, desk, carpet, and chairs. People even pulled them off each other. After ten minutes, most of the critters had been caught, except for a few that emerged from inside the grey hoodie.

The man in the suit had been called, and he followed the MLA into the office, brushing at his suit jacket and checking his pockets. He sat down as the MLA hobbled to the other side of the desk.

The man said, "I have to hand it to that woman. It must be tough to have a kid in a wheelchair like that."

"I don't think the boy in the chair is the one with the problem," the MLA said.

"Oh, of course not!" Had he said something inappropriate? Besides, who was he to argue with a man using a cane?

He looked down at his shoes. Something moved. A cricket struggled out from the confines of his pant cuff and sat on the top edge of the fabric. "Chirp!" it said, then disappeared, leaving both men awkwardly thinking of what to say next.

Chapter 15
Connecting

~~~

Mother slipped into the shower before catching a few hours of sleep prior to her next night shift. She stood under the spray, hands over her eyes, as her tears merged with the water that coursed over her. The shower was her refuge, the place where she could be alone with her fears and not worry about being judged. Here, her sounds of sorrow were drowned out by the blast of running water.

She knew her job would not last, but she tried to count her blessings: her children and the help from a friend who was always there for her. June had come over to watch the boys and get them off to school in the morning so that Mother could go to work. It was a short-term solution, but would do for now. She didn't know where she would go from here, and with that thought, she burst into another flood of tears.

While Mother found a spot for a nap, June finished washing the supper dishes in the kitchen sink. Gazing outside into the dark, her mind dwelt on the family's plight, wondering how they were going to survive.

Luke came up behind her and forced himself under her arm, looking up at her with a sad face. "I told Mom I was sorry about what happened with the crickets," he said. "I thought the bucket had apples in it. The lizards were hungry."

"Luke," June said, "you didn't have permission to open the bucket. You and your mother already had this talk about not touching things that don't belong to you."

"Do you think I'm still grounded?"

"Without a doubt, Skywalker."

"But that's not fair," he said, pouting. "How come it's always my fault? How come David never gets into trouble?"

"Because you're the one who filled the entire waiting room with bugs. "

His eyes filled with tears. "But why is it always me?"

She stroked his hair with her hand. "Well, because along with your curiosity for things, you also have opposable thumbs."

"What does that mean?" Luke asked.

"You're able to do things David is not. If he were able, he'd probably get into as much trouble as you do."

"Maybe if he wasn't disabled, Mom wouldn't hate me so much."

She felt at a loss for words—no matter what she said, she wasn't going to convince him otherwise. "Luke, your Mom is having a rough time. She needs your patience and understanding."

"Me? I'm the one getting yelled at all the time! I'm the one she's disappointed in all the time! No matter what I do, I don't do things right!"

"Luke. You *are* important. You're very special—"

"DON'T …CALL… ME… THAT!" he wailed.

June sighed, pulled him towards her and hugged him close. "I didn't mean it like that. You have your own place in your mother's heart that is just yours. You and David are different. She loves you just as much— she just shows it differently. Your brother loves you, too, and he shows it differently as well."

His tears slowed. "I don't know if he even likes me."

June felt a pain in her heart as she steered him down the hallway toward David's room, her arm still around him in a comforting hug. "I know he can't say it, Luke, but he lives and loves through you."

She pushed open the doorway to David and Mother's room, so they could both listen to David's breathing. After a moment, they also heard the distinct sound of cricket song in the darkness.

"Stowaways," June said. "They must have escaped aboard David's chair." She gestured toward the sound. "You bring him this. Through your experiences, you help your brother connect to the earth and to a world that is not quite ready for him. For that, I'm sure he's very grateful."

Luke said nothing. He gently pulled himself away from her side, walked to his room, and shut the door.

Chapter 16
Brewing

Christmas had come and gone. After the holidays, everyone had settled back into school life, including Mother. In the spring, she left the hospital emergency department, and registered at the university to take teaching courses. She felt she would be better able to provide for her family if, like the MLA had suggested, she went into a profession that she thought would have shorter hours and weekends off. She knew it would take six years as a part-time student to get her degree.

Today was Saturday, and she had to go to the library to collect books for a paper she was researching. Luke wanted to go bike riding with his friends, but Mother insisted that he stay home to help with David. As compensation, she allowed his friend, Sean, to come over to play video games.

While she got ready to leave, Goliath ran into the shoe rack at the back door, knocking boots and shoes onto the floor. As she reorganized the footwear, she discovered a case of beer that still held a few cans. Placing the empty box by the door, she put the two remaining cans in the top of an open box. She called to Julie, a lanky, fifteen-year-old neighbour who had come to babysit. "Julie, can you take this empty box out to the garbage later when you have a few minutes?"

"Sure," Julie said from the living room, where she was watching the boys play *Mario Brothers* games. She was waiting impatiently for Mother to leave so that she could use the portable phone to call her friends.

"Julie, there's leftover pizza in the fridge that you can heat up in the microwave for you and the boys. Luke will take care of David being fed. OK?"

"Yep."

"You should feed David fairly soon, Luke. He's all set up and ready to go. He just needs the formula. Luke?"

"OK!" he shouted back, as he continued to thumb the controls.

David watched the two boys play their game on the TV screen. He was only mildly interested in what they were doing, but enjoyed their conversation. He loved listening to Sean's Irish accent, and the way he said "arse." He glanced at Julie in the hope she might want to read to him, or go for a walk, or do *something*, but she didn't seem to notice he was there.

He heard his mother leave. Julie ran to the phone. Settling into a chair, she called a friend, and began talking and laughing, her legs hanging over the edge of the overstuffed living-room chair. David was caught between the boys' conversation, hooting and hollering with their game, and Julie's giggles. He rested his head, closed his eyes, and dozed off in the midst of all the chatter and television noise. There was one thing about being disabled: you could be easily ignored.

He woke to the sound of the microwave beeping and the smell of pizza. He also became aware that his stomach was rumbling. It was definitely time for lunch. He made a high-pitched screeching sound, but Luke kept on with his video game.

"Just a minute, David. I just have to beat this score. I'll get you something in a jiffy."

Julie came in with the warmed-up pizza and set the plate down in front of the boys. She returned to the kitchen, still talking on the phone, and looked out the window to see a few local boys her age passing a ball back and forth in the parking lot. She looked for Jack—he was cute. She caught sight of him, and quickly made her excuses to her friend before setting the phone down. She watched a few minutes longer, trying to think of a reason to go outside and casually parade herself in front of Jack.

A box lay by the back door, which reminded her it had to be taken to the garbage. After inspecting her image in the bathroom mirror, she picked up the box and pushed open the door, making what she thought was a grand entrance into the yard, swinging the box to make it clear she was on an important errand to the dumpster.

Jack noticed her as she exited the yard gate. She tried hard to ignore him.

Inside, Luke made good work of his game, while David waited impatiently to eat. He made the same noise again, adding the hint of a cry at the end.

"OK, OK, David. I'll get to it right away," Luke said. But he was about to beat Sean's best score, so he said, "Sean, can you grab David a can of formula from the back door and bring it in here? I don't want to stop."

Sean went to the closet and grabbed a can. He glanced out the back door and saw Julie chatting with Jack. Shaking his head, he returned to the living room. "I'm thinkin' Julie has a crush on that Jack Carter," he said.

"Really?" Luke replied absentmindedly. He looked at the can in Sean's hand and took note of the label, which read "Vanilla Flavour." "Just pop the top on it," Luke said, "and turn it over in the funnel at the top of the pole."

Sean got up on the chair and positioned the can in the way Luke had asked.

"Darn it!" Luke yelled as his Mario character lost his last life and the game ended. "Yer up, Sean, but I bet you can't beat *that* score!"

Sean took his place in front of the controls, determined to do better than Luke, but immediately botched his turn.

"I think I've got him right where I want him," Luke whispered to David. He opened the tubing, and the liquid flowed through the plastic line, dripping from the end into a small garbage can by the wheelchair. He connected the gastrostomy tube to the port that opened into David's stomach. "Mmm, good." He rubbed his stomach to suggest the flavour extended beyond the nasty smell of the liquid. David made a swallowing gesture before giving a little smile.

"Y' be up," Sean said, moving to hand him the controls.

"Hang on, I need to get David another can of food." Luke headed for the kitchen at the same time Julie yanked open the back door.

Goliath sauntered down the hallway. Seeing the open door as an invitation to go outside he seized the opportunity and jaunted past Julie into the yard. "Goliath! Back inside!" she called.

He ignored her and ventured further into the small back yard.

"Goliath, come back here!" She went after him, but he avoided her.

Luke saw through the kitchen window that she was having trouble, and went outside just as Goliath dodged Julie and headed out of the gate. She scrambled after him, frantically calling his name.

Luke stuck his head back inside. "I have to get Goliath!" he called to Sean. "Stay with David."

"Alrighty." Sean looked at David, not sure what he should do.

Luke grabbed a can from the back closet, ran to the living room, and tossed it to Sean. "Pop this in for me, will ya? Don't tell Mom I let you do this or she'll kill me." He dashed off again.

Sean popped the lid open, removed the empty can from the funnel, and replaced it with the new one. He made a face at the smell, glad he didn't have to eat it. He chatted to David, then took another turn with Mario while he waited. An extra game wouldn't hurt anything. Besides, it might give him an opportunity to catch up.

Luke ran out of the yard after Goliath, calling to him. He watched as Julie and other neighbourhood kids tried to catch the yellow retriever, who enjoyed the chase and easily avoided their attempts to grab him. Goliath finally slowed down to allow himself to be caught. At their joyous return to the house, Luke pushed the Labrador inside before him.

He came into the living room and sat down in front of the TV. "It's my turn," he said, reaching for the controls.

Sean passed them to him, looking back at David. "I gave 'im the other can o' nourish," he said in his Irish lilt.

"Thanks. Gotta keep that tummy happy, right David?" He looked back at his brother, whose face was lightly flushed.

"It surely smells awful," Sean said, holding his nose.

"I know, it's disgusting." Luke spoke quietly so as not to offend David. "But it sure makes him grow. You're right, though. It does smell worse than usual." He looked at David again. The flow was moving faster than normal, so he slowed it down.

They went back to their game, and Julie returned to her phone calls.

David felt comfortable and happy. He drooped in the chair, and found it difficult to hold his head up. Despite it being a bit of a struggle, he found that funny, and giggled to himself.

"What's so funny?" Luke asked, although his attention was mostly on his game. He heard David humming the opening bars of "Twinkle, Twinkle Little Star" and softly laughing, but passed it off and carried on with his game.

Julie entered the living room carrying a drink of water. "What's wrong with David?"

Luke looked at his brother, now hunched to one side, his face flushed, giggling and humming. Luke started toward him as the back door opened.

"I'm home!" Mother said. She set her bags by the refrigerator and dropped her keychain with a clatter onto the table.

The silence from the living room alarmed her. She felt her pulse increase, and quickened her step.

David sat leaning to one side, making noises, his face pink.

"What happened?" she asked, looking at the others. Julie shrugged her shoulders, Luke shook his head, his eyes unblinking, and Sean remained silent.

"Sweetie, what's wrong?" Mother searched David's face, and he responded with a wide smile.

Out of habit, she checked the tube attached to his stomach, and turned the flow off until she could determine what was wrong. "Did he get sick?" she asked.

"No," Luke said.

David continued humming and making silly sounds. Mother leaned forward to check his breath in case he had been sick, then became aware of a distinctive smell. She turned to the group, with one eye directed at Julie. "Has someone been drinking? I smell beer."

The trio shook their heads animatedly. "No!" they said in unison.

They all looked up at the funnel on the top of David's IV pole as his humming performance of "Itsy Bitsy Spider" became louder.

Mother reached up and pulled out a can. She held it up: it bore a Canadian Maple Leaf.

Julie quickly disappeared into the kitchen and Sean returned to the video game, pretending to be engrossed in the action, hoping his mother would arrive soon to take him home.

Luke stood in front of Mother, terrified, watching her expression change from worry to anger. "How could you be so careless?"

"I got the formula from the box at the back!" he said, tears forming in his eyes.

The mental image of a beer case at the back door brusquely reminded her of her negligence in not putting the remaining cans in the fridge. "Didn't you look at the can when you picked it up?"

"Goliath got outside and was running around in the parking lot, and I was in a hurry to get him."

Mother unstrapped David from his chair, and carried him into the bedroom. She lay him down onto his bed and turned him onto his left side so that he would be in less danger if he got sick. He continued humming his repertoire: he was halfway through "Shoo Fly."

Mother returned to the kitchen to find Dr. Liam's number, stopping in front of the refrigerator door, which was covered with about forty medically related business cards. Each contained the name of a doctor, medical business, agency, social worker, or specialist. They were arranged in alphabetical order. She drew her finger across them until she came to Dr. Liam's name. The number should have been emblazoned in her memory, but panic had erased it.

Chapter 17
Worrying

Dr. Liam returned Mother's call while on his hospital rounds. "What's the problem?"

She kept her fears from surfacing, while aware of the anxiety in her voice. "I don't know how to explain this, but Luke accidentally gave David half a can of beer via his G-tube."

"Good God. How did he manage that?"

"It's a long story. At any rate, how much danger is David in? Do I need to bring him into the hospital?

"How long ago was it?"

"By the rate of the flow, I'd say over an hour or so. He hasn't been sick."

"If he's not getting sick, he's probably fine," Dr. Liam said. "But keep an eye on him in case he vomits. We don't want him to aspirate any liquid into his lungs."

"Is there anything else I can do?"

"Sure, make him a strong cup of coffee."

"What?"

"I'm joking. What about Luke?"

"He's in trouble, that's what."

"Put him on."

Luke took the phone and said a weak hello. David's well-being was compromised, and it was his fault yet again.

"Poole, I hear you got your brother drunk."

Luke swallowed, unable to respond.

"Look, there's no way you would have done that on purpose," Dr. Liam said. "I don't know the details, but I know it had to have been an accident, and it isn't your fault. David will be fine. Heck, in the long run, you probably did him a favour." He laughed softly. "What's he doing right now?"

"He's humming 'Happy Birthday.'"

Dr. Liam's laughter exploded. "Let me talk to your mother again. Everything will be fine, Luke. Don't worry."

Mother grabbed the phone from Luke, glaring at him.

"You know, I hate to say this, but sometimes I think you give that kid too much responsibility," Dr. Liam said to her. "I know you need help, but he's really only a boy."

She felt a pang of guilt, looking down at one distraught child and another overly cheerful one. "I'm aware of that," she said, slightly annoyed. "But if you know of somebody willing to take on this responsibility at a moment's notice for a couple of bucks an hour, I'll hire them." Changing the subject, she asked, "Is there anything else I should do for David?"

"Don't forget there are agencies. I know your choices are limited, but you have to work with what you have. In answer to your question, you could give him some Tylenol."

"Do you think he's in pain?"

"No, it's for the hangover that's probably on its way," Dr. Liam said. She rolled her eyes.

"Page me if you have any more concerns," he said before hanging up.

Mother turned off the phone and slid her hand over David's forehead. He closed his eyes as if he were about to take a nap. She called to Julie to bring her the bottle of liquid Tylenol and a syringe. Still feeling angry, she kept her eyes on David and away from Luke.

"I'm sorry," Luke said with tears in his eyes.

"Let's not talk about this right now," she said, controlling her voice. "Go visit with Sean. We'll talk about it later."

He returned to the living room and sat with his friend. He worried about what might happen to David, and about what would happen to him.

But nothing happened. They never spoke of it again.

Chapter 18
Parking

Spring always carried the threat of a snowfall, even in late May. Nonetheless, plants were encouraged to poke their heads up from the ground, and noisy magpies lined fences, squawking their early-morning songs in the temporary sunshine.

In the back yard, a lilac tree struggled to grow in a shaded area of the garden, but it still produced milk-white flowers that exuded a pleasing, calming scent. Luke stood beside the small tree, pulling at a section of blooms to remove it from the branch. He buried his face in the star-shaped flowers, taking in the perfume, then placed the garland under his brother's nose. David took a breath in and responded with an eager smile.

"That's not a good idea," Mother said. "He's probably allergic."

"How can you tell? He's always coughing and sneezing."

"True, but he seems to have a bit of a cold now, so let's not make things worse." She pulled out her dragon-shaped metal keychain, its swinging movement reflecting the sunlight. She opened the gate to let Luke push David through to the van. They loaded him aboard, then strapped his chair to the floor. Luke buckled himself in before she drove out onto the street, heading the several blocks to the grocery store.

She glanced in the rearview mirror at Luke sitting passively in his seat. He appeared moody—a common state of late. "Did I tell you we're meeting Beth and Christopher Crispen at the grocers? That will be nice. You haven't seen Chris in a while."

"Yeah, I have," Luke said. "I see him at school. He's in the same class as David and I've talked to him a few times when I've gone to see David."

She nodded in acknowledgement as she pulled into the grocery parking lot. The lot was jammed, except for one handicap stall at one end. The spot was filled with abandoned grocery carts that hadn't yet been picked up by an attendant. She stopped the van, blocking traffic, so that she could move the carts out of the way. She called to Luke for help, but he didn't budge from his seat. After pushing the carts to their proper spot, she climbed back into the van, a foul mood following her.

Luke exited out the front passenger door. "I see Chris!" he said, closing the door.

Mother closed her eyes tightly and drew in a deep breath to calm herself. She got David out and proceeded toward the shop doors, where she greeted Beth and Chris and averted her eyes from Luke. *Let it go*, she kept telling herself. She touched Chris's shoulder to acknowledge him, and he raised his right arm in a welcoming gesture. Like David, he was unable to speak, and depended on his family for daily needs. But, also like David, he had a cheerful, friendly smile, and a pleasant disposition.

Beth riffled through her bag, retrieving a cigarette pack. She was a small, slight woman, with a tough exterior and thick, curly hair. She lit a cigarette and took a few puffs before going into the supermarket. It had been several hours since her last opportunity to light up.

As the women chatted about their morning, a few people exited the store, and turned to stare with somber faces at the group. Mother's previous annoyance bubbled with added intensity. "Do you ever get used to the staring?" she asked in a low voice.

"Maybe Chris has," Beth said, "but I can't say I have. Most times we ignore it, but sometimes it gets the best of me and I react. It depends."

"How do you react?"

"With the ruder ones, sometimes I do something to make a point. It's not right, but at times I get fed up and do something to protest."

Mother believed that most people didn't sit in judgement, but she also knew what Beth meant. Disability scared many people, and she felt it was partly her responsibility to educate them on how well her son adapted to social norms. How well social norms adapted to him was another matter.

Beth drew on her cigarette. A man passed them and did a double take as he caught sight of the children, and of Beth with the cigarette between her fingers. He stared at her, his expression one of puzzlement, with a hint of disgust.

Mother shuffled her feet, and watched Beth crush her cigarette into the receptacle and then pull out a new one. She placed it in between Chris's fingers. Through the side of her mouth, she muttered, "Say hi, Chris." He raised his arm in salutation to the gawking man. Beth pulled out her lighter and struck the flint, as if to light the cigarette in her son's hand.

The man recoiled. He stomped past the group, glaring his dismay and disapproval. Beth snapped the lighter shut and pulled the unlit cigarette from Chris' hand. She threw the lighter and the cigarette into her bag. "In answer to your question, sometimes I do things like that," she said matter-of-factly.

The women broke into laughter as they moved everyone inside.

Chapter 19
Dodging

Beth pushed Chris with one hand, towing a shopping cart with the other. Mother carried a basket while Luke pushed David, jerking the chair to a quick stop every few steps to make him squeal with excitement.

"What do you need to get?" Beth asked.

"Whatever's on sale," replied Mother. It was easier to budget that way. When she ran out of money, she stopped buying things. She still called it budgeting.

"Did you hear about what happened to Anna and Eric?"

Mother checked the price on a box of oranges. They were on sale, and she could see why. "No. What's happened?"

"Well, they've had Jaden in a segregated program for children with high needs for the past six years," Beth said.

Mother nodded. She was familiar with the family, and David had been in the program for a while when he was younger. It was an exclusive program for medically fragile children who did not benefit from a regular school curriculum. It was not academically focused. Instead, it catered to the more demanding needs of the children in attendance. The program was executed by teachers, but also addressed sensory, gross-motor and fine-motor skills. The team included occupational therapists, physical therapists, speech pathologists, a seating team, a feeding team, nurses, and a whole host of other professionals, all on-site, for children with complex needs. Like most school programs, it struggled to meet the demands of an ever-increasing population of delicate children with little money and a significant turnover in staff.

"Anna got a letter from the school board insisting that she register Jaden in a regular school program," Beth continued.

"Uh-huh, the inclusion push. Is he in an adapted classroom?" Mother asked.

"No. He was put in a regular eighth-grade classroom, taking regular classes like language arts, science, and math. They told her he would get an educational aide who would adjust the program to meet his learning needs, but that he should be in a regular school program like any other kid."

"But he's not like any other kid," Mother said. "Most of his needs are physical, and he's prone to outbursts. The aide is going to spend all day toileting him, feeding him, providing physical therapy, or pushing him up and down the hall to quiet him. He's not going to read or do math anyway. It's ridiculous. How are the other kids in the classroom supposed to cope?"

"I know," Beth said. "Supposedly he's shortchanged if not included in a regular classroom. They believe he has a right to be part of the 'community.'" She traced quotation marks in the air. "They've got a ramp and a handicapped door opener at the front of the school, so they think they're prepared."

Mother shook her head in irritation. "He needs to be where his needs are best met. What about partial integration like David and Chris?"

"Nope. The powers-that-be decided Jaden was going into a regular Grade 8 program. It lasted about a month before it was obvious they couldn't accommodate him and that he needed to be moved to a different site—the only problem was that there was nowhere to move him to. He'd lost his spot in the segregated program, so Anna and Eric had to remove him from the school."

"Perfect," Mother said derisively. "Then what?"

"Anna had to take a leave of absence from her job and stay home to look after him. They're still looking for a program to put him in. The waiting list could be up to three years. Now they're living on Eric's income, and are afraid they won't make their mortgage payments. They're sick with worry."

Mother looked at Beth, feeling accustomed disbelief and resignation. "It's such a shame."

"I signed up for a home program for Chris when he was born," Beth said. "It was offered to severely disabled children when they turned one, and continued until they were three. We were on the waiting list for two and a half years—in the end, we got the service for six months. The most useful programs are always the ones that lack sufficient support. You'd think parents' knowledge about the welfare of their children would be worth something and considered in the decision about where they should be schooled."

The words were all too familiar, and Mother nodded her head in agreement. "Luke has been in classes with special-needs students who unintentionally disrupt the learning of others. Parents on both sides need to be considered. Regular kids should have a positive learning space, too. I'm so glad for the program David is in right now. He's in a regular program for music and art, but in his own classroom for the adapted learning. I feel lucky that I got him in when I did. My only worry is what to do when he's eighteen. The options are slim to none."

"I know." Beth looked at her son. "That worries me, too." Her mind wandered to a news story she had read recently about an elderly mother who had shut herself and her adult son in a closet and taken both their lives. Her note explained that her desperation arose from the belief there would be no one to look after him if anything happened to her.

As the group plodded along, the cart and basket beginning to fill, Luke and David grew impatient. David fretted in his chair, wanting more action, or at least more adventurous movement.

"Mom, can I take David for a walk through the store?" Luke said.

Mother hesitated. "You can, but don't wander too far from us. Why don't you stop by the pharmacy to see if his meds are ready? Wait for us there."

Luke gave David's chair a heavy push and, with a shriek of joy from his curly-haired brother, they were off. He steered the chair down an aisle, and made sudden stops that jolted David forward, making them both laugh all the harder. The chair screeched around a corner as Luke avoided getting in the way of other customers. "Hey!" Luke said. "Wanna play dodge-a-pole?"

David turned his head to look at Luke. He knew the game from an earlier time when they were shopping at a mall in the southeast section of the city. A large walking space covered the centre, with shops on either side. Within the centre was another strip that held small kiosks, benches, garbage cans, and the Information Centre. Flanking each side of the centre strip were large columns, three meters apart, which stretched down the length of the walkway. David and Luke got lots of stares but, at the same time, they'd noticed that while people stared, they also ran into the poles. Some were able to dodge the poles, but most walked directly into them, whacking the poles. On that day, they counted five people hitting the poles, three dodging them, four running into garbage cans, and one falling over a bench. Oftentimes, when the scene involved a child, the crash was preceded by a question. "Mom, what's wrong with that boy?" If the question was ignored, the child inevitably connected with an immobile object.

Luke looked for a candidate. A young girl their age came down the shopping aisle behind her parents. She had a lollypop in her mouth and seemed distracted. An abandoned shopping basket sat on the floor on her side of the aisle. "What do you think, David?" Luke asked. "Whack, or dodge-a-pole?"

David remained still, making no sound.

"That would be a no. Dodge-a-pole then?"

"Yah," David responded.

"Really, dude? She hasn't even seen us yet. I think she'll hit the basket."

As they watched, their eyes met the girl's. A puzzled look came over her face. She had almost reached the basket, but before Luke could call out a warning, she side-stepped the obstacle and kept going. She glanced back for a second, still working the candy in her mouth, before turning the corner and vanishing from sight.

"You won that round, David. You can sure read 'em. But we should get a move on. Let's go get your bags of meds."

At the pharmacy counter, Luke asked if David's supplies were ready. The pharmacist placed two large paper bags, a few large economy-sized containers, and an assortment of small bags filled with pill bottles into a waiting grocery cart. He slid a large box of diapers from behind the counter and put it in as well. "This should do you for a few weeks, David," the pharmacist said. "Is your mom here?"

"Yes. She should be here to pay for it in a minute," Luke replied. "We're just going to look down the cookie aisle. I hear Mr. Christie calling my name."

"I also hear they have a special on chocolate mallow cookies," the pharmacist replied with a wink.

Luke and David cruised along, looking for the cookies. They saw a boy their age examining the bags on the shelf. A woman pushing a cart, two more children hanging off its sides, was about to disappear around the corner at the end of the aisle.

"Ethan, hurry up!" They heard the woman's words shouted in their direction. Ethan ignored the shout to look the boys over. They had stopped beside him while searching for Luke's favourite chocolate-chip cookies.

"What's the matter with him?" Ethan asked, motioning in David's direction.

Luke looked into the boy's inquisitive pale-blue eyes. He looked back at his brother, and gave him a quick once-over. David's nose was running after his previous sneeze. Luke pulled his jacket sleeve over his hand and wiped under David's nose. "Nothing really, he has a bit of a cold." He looked back at Ethan.

The other boy had an odd look on his face. "No. That's not what I meant. What's *wrong* with him?"

"Oh, you mean, what's his *condition*?"

Ethan shrugged.

"My brother has what's called cerebral palsy. He was born with it because he was born too early, but we don't know why. It was just one of those things. He can't talk or walk, but he can understand what you're saying. He's pretty bright, if I do say so myself. Say hi, David."

In response to Luke's request, David flashed a smile and breathed out a soft sound. "Hi."

The cart with the two kids hanging off of it had reappeared at the end of the aisle. "Ethan! Get over here—*now!*" the woman shouted, annoyance stamped on her voice. Ethan hurried away with neither a word nor backward glance, and disappeared around the corner.

"Luke!" Mother's voice called from the opposite end of the aisle. "You were supposed to wait for us at the pharmacy. We're ready to go to the checkout now."

Luke grabbed the bag of cookies, and flung it into David's lap, thinking he was worth a bag of cookies, at least. But in the checkout line, Mother removed the cookies from her basket and tossed them aside to be returned. Luke's face dropped. His look of dismay and hurt transformed into anger as he made his way out of the building.

Once outside, avoiding goodbyes to Chris and Beth, Luke stood by the van door, waiting to be let in. Mother asked him to help with David, and to put the shopping bags inside Smog. He shuffled over, feeling sullen.

"That's enough," she said.

Luke reacted. "Really? Really? Yes! It *is* enough, Mom! I'm brought along like some kind of slave to help out all the time, and you can't even get me a bag of cookies!"

"I don't have the money for it right now!"

"Yeah, right. But all of the bags in the van are for David. Why is it never about me?"

"It's not the same!"

"I know it's not the same! I hear it over and over and over!"

They both felt distraught and unable to hold back tears. They stood facing each other, neither aware of their public surroundings, until a friendly voice spoke. "I just thought I'd let you know that we can hear you two from across the parking lot." June was walking toward them, smiling, with Rayne a few feet behind her. "Let me give you a hand with this," she continued, grabbing the large box of diapers off of the cart. "Rayne, why don't you take Luke back to their house? We'll meet you there."

Rayne nodded, and waited for Luke to join him. Luke pushed his hands down into his pockets and shambled off in the direction of Rayne's car.

June turned to Mother, like the calm of a warm spring day. They waited until they were inside the van before they began to talk. Mother still felt engulfed in anger. "I don't know what I'm supposed to do with him!"

"You said you couldn't afford the cookies. I get that. But was there something else he could have had instead?" June asked.

"He doesn't deserve anything special based on his behaviour lately!"

"Ah, so it wasn't about the money. You told him it was about the money. I understand that Luke hasn't been the easiest person to get along with lately, but you weren't honest with him."

"I told him he couldn't have it. That should be enough."

"I'm trying to say that if there was a lesson behind this, I don't think he knew it. It sounds like he thinks you wouldn't let him have the cookies because you don't care about what he wants."

Mother shoved the van into gear. "You know, June, I realize you mean well, but maybe you just need to stay out of this." She drove out of the parking lot. The iciness in the air was hard to ignore.

Chapter 20
Thinking

Alone in the car with Rayne, Luke turned his head toward the window and cried. Rayne said nothing, and pulled out into the traffic. Luke soon started to pour out his heart, but Rayne didn't know what he was saying. He knew there were words in there, but the sobbing blotted them out.

They continued past Luke's block until they came to a small, quiet park at the side of the road—an oasis in the middle of chaos. There was a bench a few yards in, beside a narrow sidewalk that wound through a wooded area.

Rayne reached into the glove compartment and pulled out a wad of A&W napkins, several of which he handed to Luke. He waited until Luke looked calm enough to talk, then suggested they sit on the bench and listen to the sounds of the park—birds, the breeze, or people calling to their dogs.

Once outside in the fresh air, Luke appeared calmer. He kicked at the stones under the bench as he swung his feet back and forth. "I hate my life," he blurted out. "I hate that nobody cares about me."

Rayne nodded his head, but said nothing.

"You know what I mean, don't you?"

Rayne nodded again.

"How am I supposed to fix this? How am I suppose to matter to anyone? David gets all the attention and I get nothing! If we buy something, it's for David. If we go somewhere, it's for David. If plans are changed, it's because of David. What am I supposed to do?"

"I don't know," Rayne said, not looking at Luke. "Sounds to me like you need to be in a wheelchair."

Luke stopped and stared at him. "That's stupid."

Rayne agreed. "Yes, it is. I don't know anything about how this feels, but, you have cats, right?"

"Well...yeah. Montgomery and Bronte."

"How often do you take the cats for a walk?"

"Whaaaaat?"

"All right. The answer is you don't, 'cause they don't need walks. How often do you take Goliath out for a walk?"

"Every day."

"Right. Because he needs to go for a walk. The cats aren't complaining that no one is taking them for a walk. "

"Are you for real?"

"Look, what I'm trying to say is you can't treat everyone the same, because they're not the same. You just have to be fair."

"But I'm not being treated fair!"

"I don't know, Luke. Maybe you just aren't being treated the way you want. David can't do what you do and that's not fair, but that's the way it is."

Luke huffed and sat back on the bench, listening to the birds singing. "What bird is that?" he asked after a moment.

"I don't know."

"Why don't you know?"

"Why should I know?"

"Cause I thought you'd know."

"It's a quail."

"For sure?"

"No idea." Rayne bumped Luke with his elbow, then stood up and headed in the direction of the car.

"Why don't you know?" Luke asked, following him.

"Because I don't." Rayne laughed. "You think I'm supposed to know because I'm old, or because I'm Indian?"

"Well...both."

"Let's think about this for a minute," Rayne said. "You figure I know bird sounds 'cause I'm native. People think David's life is horrible because he's disabled. People think your mother is a saint because she's handling all this alone. They also think your life is wonderful because you're healthy and have all your fingers and toes. Funny thing is, all of those things are wrong. I know nothing about birds; they don't interest me at all. David is waited on hand-and-foot like a prince and has a stress-free, happy life, when he's well. Your mother is an emotional wreck and struggles every day to stay sane. You're the most miserable kid I know, and you have no real reason to be."

Luke looked at him silently and blinked several times.

"Luke, the only person who can really make you feel good about yourself is you. You have to earn your own love and respect. Don't waste your time testing other people for it."

"I don't know what you mean."

"Pay attention to what you do, and do the things that make you proud of yourself. Don't judge your worth on how you think others see you." They arrived at the car, and Rayne pulled open the door.

"I'm still not sure I get it," Luke said. He got into the passenger seat.

Rayne shrugged. "Just keep thinking about it. It's all about the learning."

"Learning? Hey, you could teach me how to drive, right? That would be learning."

"Wrong!" Rayne slammed the passenger door and walked around to the driver's side. "Kids," he muttered to himself. He stopped and listened to the bird sounds again. "Is it a robin? Maybe a sparrow?"

A motorcycle sped by. "Harley," he said confidently as he dropped himself into the driver's seat, and started the engine.

Chapter 21
Juggling

~~~~~~~~~~~~~~~~

It was almost summer. Mother struggled to keep up with the demands of her part-time university courses while continuing to look after her sons. She had been up most of the night finishing a paper, a common occurrence over the past few weeks. In addition, David called for help every few hours, to be changed or turned. Physically and mentally exhausted, she ran on coffee and adrenalin, like most students.

She stared absentmindedly at the pile of hand-printed pages, uncertain whether her argument made sense. There should be ways she could save enough money to invest in a typewriter with a self-correct ribbon to make her job easier. She knew of a few people who had their own computers, but they took up so much space, and were too expensive.

She held the pink and gold-lettered "#1 Mom" coffee mug donated to her at a garage sale by someone she didn't even know. She lifted the ceramic mug to her mouth, but it was empty. A burning sensation in her stomach signaled that she had reached her limit of caffeine abuse, and needed food.

Luke, tousle-haired and sleepy-eyed, appeared in the doorway. He seemed to be in a good mood. From the end of the hall, she heard a succession of bird-like twitters, followed by an excited squawking sound.

She headed toward David's room. "Luke, grab yourself a bowl of cereal before school," she said on her way. "Check the milk before you pour."

Luke sank into Mother's chair. Still waiting for his brain to waken, he hung his head backwards over the chair, and looked up at the collection of cobwebs in the corners of the ceiling. *Those aren't just webs*, he thought, *those are communities. Doesn't she clean?*

When he finished breakfast, he got himself dressed and ready for school. Mother brought David down the hallway to the front door, and began pushing his arms into his jacket. As soon as she had all his straps in place and his backpack hanging at the rear of his chair, she heard the blast of the bus horn.

"We're going out for dinner tonight, Luke, so make sure you get your homework done right after school," she said. "Chris and his Mom will be there too. Now let's get going or I'll be late. I have schoolwork to hand in this morning."

"Why don't you give it to them tomorrow?"

Mother grabbed an elastic and twisted it around her uncombed hair, to drag it out of her face. "Hand it in late? No. That's irresponsible. Besides, I have exams to study for."

"Why don't you play hooky?"

"I pay a lot of money to go to school, Luke. I'm not playing hooky. And by the way, how do you know about hooky?"

"Um. *Ferris Buhler's Day Off.*"

"I see."

The trio headed down the sidewalk toward David's bus. Gear sounds assaulted the morning quiet as the lift opened out and the bus's jaw dropped to the ground to receive him. A moment later, Luke's bus arrived at the corner, and Mother watched as he ran toward the open door. He turned back for a quick wave, then was swallowed by the yellow vessel. A sea of heads bobbed in the windows, but none of them were Luke's. *He must be on the other side*, she thought, but waved just in case.

She went back into the house to get ready; there wasn't much time. She would take the bus to the university rather than do the twenty-minute bike ride. She often rode her bike in the summer, not only because it was quicker, but because a parking pass or plugging a meter was too expensive. At least on the bus she might get a thirty-minute snooze before classes. It had been nearly forty-eight hours since she had slept properly, and eleven years since the birth of her eldest son, which was the last time she had had a full night's sleep without interruption. Even with occasional respite care on weekends, she never seemed to catch up on her sleep. David's needs and restlessness at night took priority. Over the years, sleep deprivation had manifested into irritability, impatience, sensitivity, and forgetfulness. Still, she focused her energies on the possibility of an evening out while she got herself ready to go. It would be great to take the boys out for dinner.

She scrubbed her face with soap and water, zipped up her jacket, and slung her heavy backpack over her shoulders. She looked up at the empty key hook by the door. "Damn it, where the hell are my keys?"

She threw her backpack on the floor and started to cry, fatigue taking its toll. She had no idea where her keys were, and the thought of looking for them was too taxing. *Luke! Where did he put them?*

As abruptly as she had started crying when her despair had overtaken her, she stopped, and began searching desperately through her bag. She spotted them on the edge of the coffee table, right where she had left them. She grabbed them and her pack and ran out the door, locking it behind her.

The paper! Do I have my term paper? She unlocked the door again and made a mad dash to the kitchen table, only to find her paper on how behaviourists and psychoanalysts differ in their theories on hysteria still lying there. The pages were hastily zipped into her backpack as she ran out the door, locking it behind her again. She reached into her pocket for her bus pass, and found it missing. A succession of swear words led her back inside once more, where she searched anxiously until she located it. Locking the door behind her, she ran as hard as she could to the nearby bus stop. Black smoke from the exhaust pipe spewed out at her as the bus pulled away. Out of breath and patience, she sat down on the bench and did the only thing she thought herself capable of doing: she publicly and unabashedly cried her eyes out and waited for the next bus.

Chapter 22
Suffering

After school that same day, Luke reviewed his weekly spelling words, and tried to print them out on a piece of paper on the kitchen floor. David lay on a mat in the living room, watching TV, while Mother sat at the kitchen table, pencil in hand, reading a textbook. She jotted notes in the corners of the pages as she read. Examining her image in the mirror earlier, she'd thought she looked more rested than she had that morning—less grey in the face, and with fewer deep creases around her mouth. She had grabbed a quick nap before they got home.

Luke got up from his chair and pulled open the refrigerator door. He stared at the contents inside. "There's nothing in here to eat," he said.

"You mean there isn't any junk food."

"No. There is nothing good in here to eat."

"Have some fruit."

"It's all squishy," he replied, dropping a wrinkled apple back into the fruit basket on the counter.

"We're going for dinner right away, so let's get David ready to go. You can have something to eat when we get there."

Luke felt hungry right then, so he grabbed a mandarin orange. It was soft, and looked overripe. He pushed the squishy piece of fruit into his jacket pocket, and went to get David's chair.

Mother had lifted David up from the floor, and was about to place him in his wheelchair when she noticed something on the seat. He was heavy, but she knew how to compensate for the weight without compromising her back. "Luke, there's something wet on David's chair, probably a formula spill. Quick now, wipe it off. I can't hold him much longer."

Luke looked around for a towel, but the only absorbent article within reach was his jacket. He laid it down over David's chair to soak up the spill, knowing he could grab his other jacket if this one got too wet. Before he had a chance to retrieve it, Mother sat David back down on the seat. She pulled herself upright, checking to ensure there had been no strain to her lower back. "Sorry about your coat, Luke, but I'm not going to move him again to get it out. Grab your other one."

David looked confused, and reached out his arm to touch her. "Mummmmm."

She continued to buckle him in, unaware that he was trying to get her attention.

Luke came back into the living room as she was pushing David out the door. He reached out his hand to touch Luke. "Mummmmm."

"We're going for a car ride, buddy. Keep your hands and arms inside the carpet!" he said, quoting the film *Aladdin*.

David continued to sound the word, but Mother was too absorbed in her driving to pay attention.

When they arrived at Ming's Chinese restaurant, a vehicle with a handicapped sticker was parked in the only available stall, which shared ramp access to the sidewalk. The driver was surely mobile, since the car was parked in such a way that it only let pedestrians through, blocking wheelchairs and strollers. Mother's only option was to ask for help lifting her son and the heavy wheelchair onto the sidewalk.

Inside, everyone in their party had begun to arrive, adding up to a grand total of ten at the table. Some sat in wooden chairs, others in wheelchairs, and some in strollers. Everyone enjoyed the visit and the variety of food served. Luke loved using chopsticks, but even pretending they were drumsticks and snapping out a drum roll didn't amuse David, whose agitation only increased. Luke gently rocked the wheelchair, and the movement worked for a short time.

As topics changed, the group remained happy and engaged. Walter, who was a portly fellow in his fifties with a receding hairline and bushy brows, sat next to Mother and made polite conversation. He was a computer analyst by trade. He asked what courses she was taking, and how she was balancing university studies with home life.

She explained a paper she had to write for a philosophy course. The assignment felt close to home, and she was struggling with it. Her research and remarks addressed the response to the tragic story of Robert Latimer and his daughter, Tracy. As she recounted the events surrounding the story, others stopped to listen. Despite its having happened a few years earlier, it had remained an uneasy topic that did not rest well with most parents of disabled children.

"Rather than struggle with it, why not just say how you feel about it?" Walter asked.

"I'm trying to do that, but it hits so close to home. Still, I don't want to cop out on the assignment, either."

"Is he that guy who killed his daughter because she was disabled?" The question came from the teenaged daughter of a family at the table.

"More or less," Mother said. "It was referred to as a compassionate homicide. He did what he thought he needed to do to stop her suffering. The trouble I have with it is, how did he know she was suffering? She couldn't tell him. How can you measure for someone else what a quality of life is or isn't? All you can go on is your own interpretation, based on your own values, and if you don't value it, you probably don't support it."

"I have an issue with it too, for the poor wee girl." Karen, the mother of a child with a rare genetic disorder, held up her hand as she spoke. "But more so, I have a problem with how much support he got. Some people look at our kids and think about how they'd feel if they switched places. You can't do that. What our kids are is all they know. They don't miss an experience they never had, like playing with a Barbie, or being captain of a baseball team. Like Walter, here. I'm sure he misses his calling as a professional ice dancer." She winked in Walter's direction.

Walter snickered in good humour, then said, "You play the hand you're dealt. What's important for my daughter is to have opportunities for new experiences, to be loved, and to laugh. This may sound odd, but who she is now is just fine with her mother and me. If God were to come down and say, 'How about I fix this and make her like a normal kid?' I know I'd say, "Wait a minute...give me a second to think about that. I like *this* kid."

Most of the parents exchanged looks of understanding.

Luke had slowed his rocking movement, and David's fussing had returned. He whimpered his distress, and his mouth dropped into a deep frown. He began to wail. Mother moved over to see if she could figure out what was wrong. She repositioned his straps, which didn't help. He couldn't be hungry, since he had recently been fed. His forehead felt cool, so he didn't have a fever. She didn't smell anything that indicated an accident, and had changed him before coming out. Besides, public changing facilities mostly accommodated babies, not larger children, and she was hoping not to have to put him on the dirty floor in the bathroom. She would change him on the floor in the van if necessary, or take him home.

Other people in the restaurant appeared to be listening to the conversation without contributing their thoughts on the subject. They simply glanced with curiosity in the group's direction.

"I'm still not sure what angle to take in writing my paper," Mother said, returning her attention to the group. "How do I defend our children and question the notion he was a type of folk hero who acted out of love?"

"Why not compare him to someone else who recently murdered her children. She also believed it was the right thing to do." said Diane, a mother of three who also owned her own grocery store.

"Who are you thinking of?"

"Andrea Yates."

Mother acknowledged the name. She was aware that Yates had drowned her five children in the bathtub. Her defense was that she did it out of love, to save them from suffering through a divorce and the disruption of being separated from her. In reality, Yates likely had a psychiatric problem. She had immediately been called "a baby murderer," while Robert Latimer's friends and family had taken up a collection for his defense, and treated him like a selfless hero.

"So what do you think is the main difference between the two situations?" Karen asked.

"Simply put, it's about what society values," replied Beth.

Mother stabbed the air to show her accord. "And if the courts don't treat him as a criminal, and he doesn't do the time required for the act he committed, it puts our children's value and safety into question."

"I think you have your paper," Walter said.

She sat back, allowing the ideas to run through her head.

David had reached full crying mode, and nothing she did settled him. As a last resort, she packed up everything, made her excuses to her friends, and headed for Smog, parked down the street.

Passing another table, she overheard a diner's comment. "That poor child must be in such pain." She dismissed it, and continued toward the outside, where she loaded David into the van. She managed awkwardly to pull him out of the chair and lay him on the floor. As she turned him onto his side, she saw that the back of his pants were wet. He wore a disposable diaper; the outside should be dry. An odd smell drifted through the car, and she went back to the chair, where she pulled up Luke's jacket. A wet stain covered one of the pockets, which appeared to be filled. She reached inside and pulled out a flattened piece of orange flesh and peel.

"Seriously?" she said to Luke. "You put an orange in your jacket before you put it down on David's chair?"

"I didn't do it on purpose!"

"But Luke, you didn't think! You never stop to think about how your actions affect David!"

"Here we go again! It's always about David and never about Luke! Sometimes I hate him! Sometimes I wish he'd never been born!"

They stood outside the van on the sidewalk. Her reaction was swift and immediate. She slapped his face. "Dammit, Luke! You know he understands you!" she said in a furious whisper.

Luke burst into tears and stamped his way into the van, slamming the door. Mother stood alone, feeling shaken and remorseful. Tears ran down her cheeks as she struggled with what she had done. Should she just walk away right then? Giving up wasn't defeat; it was sensible. Maybe she could start down the sidewalk and keep going. Who would notice anyway? Who would care? Her guts felt raw, and she had no idea what she would say. She knew the battle wasn't over, but she had no will and no idea how to fight it anymore.

She climbed in and pulled the driver's door shut behind her. Still struggling with tears, she said, "Luke, I'm sorry. That should never have happened, and I promise you it will never happen again. Something has to change. Please know that I love both of you with all my heart. I want no harm to come to either of you. You boys are my life."

Luke stared out the window, tears still coursing down his face. He couldn't look at her, not because he was still angry or hurt, but because what he had said about his brother ate at him. He'd apologized the moment he had gotten inside, but it hadn't made him feel better. He had noticed David staring at his motionless hands with an expressionless face. *She's right. We can't stay here. Something has to change.*

Chapter 23
Beating

Luke awoke at midnight to a braying sound coming from David's room. He wandered into the hallway to see Goliath and the two cats skittering down the hall into the living room. Mother must have fallen asleep on the couch while studying. He flicked on the light; both cats bounced eagerly on her to waken her. Goliath stood dutifully at the bottom of the sofa, waiting for her to go to David.

The scene was familiar enough. David could accurately sense when he had a fever, and begin making the tell-tale sound whenever his temperature rose to 38 degrees, only one degree higher than normal. They all headed for David and Mother's bedroom, except Luke, who ran to get the portable phone.

Bronte, the calico cat, settled herself close to David's head, as if she knew he had a fever. Montgomery sat at David's feet, her keen eyes on him. Goliath positioned himself on the floor, out of the way at the end of the bed, but close enough to be of help. It was a family affair.

Mother placed a tympanic thermometer in David's ear and pressed the trigger. It registered 43 degrees. She slid her hand over his flushed face, and felt the intensity of the heat. She pulled her stethoscope off of the IV pole and listened to his chest. The noise of his breathing was not unlike a percolating coffee pot. The sound suggested a severe chest infection.

Goliath pulled a washcloth off the supply shelf by the door and held it in his mouth. Mother ran it under cold water in the bathroom. She returned, placed it on David's forehead, and then went to find Ibuprofen to break the fever.

She was fully awake and in crisis mode, an accustomed state. As the seriousness of the situation rose, she forced herself to stay calm and controlled enough to make rational and split-second decisions. It took energy.

"Luke, can you get dressed? We need to get your brother to the hospital. He's having trouble breathing."

"Are we going by ambulance?"

"No, it costs too much and he should be at the South Side Hospital where Dr. Liam can see him. The ambulance dispatchers always decide which hospital he should go to, depending on how busy the emergency departments are. But if they take him somewhere else, Dr. Liam can't treat him, and then he's with someone who doesn't know him. Besides, the driver won't take his chair, and we need it." She knew she was taking a risk not calling for an ambulance, but it was one she had to take.

In the hospital emergency department, the triage nurse took David's vital signs, then moved him into the trauma room, where he was transferred to a stretcher. The trauma team hooked him up to Ventolin by mask to improve his breathing, and started an IV. A nurse stuck a series of leads onto his chest and body to monitor his heart. The TV screen above him provided information on his blood pressure, heart rate, oxygen saturation level, and heart rhythm. A bell rang when the levels were dangerously high or low. It rang frequently.

The trauma room was set up with two monitors: one above where the patient lay, and the other on the opposite side, close to where the nurses did their charting. David's nurse worked at a bedside table, and had positioned it for a clear view of one of the monitors. His back was to Mother and the boys. When the warning bell rang, he glanced up to make sure the rhythms remained within a reasonable limit.

Mother sat on a chair near David's head, and Luke pulled up a chair on the other side. David appeared agitated and scared, making various sounds, and striking his arms in the air while kicking his legs under the sheet that covered him. Mother tried to settle him by talking and stroking his forehead, but he was too upset, and continued to make noise and flail his limbs. She tried singing softly to him, but his agitation continued. He began to hyperventilate. As a last resort, she lightly pounded the centre of his chest with a cupped hand, making a clopping sound, not unlike the rhythm of a horse's hooves. The sound was obliterated by the noises of other machines and monitors in the room, and David's nurse was unaware that Mother was giving her son chest physio. In certain circumstances, this action had proved to settle him down because it loosened the phlegm in his chest or, at the very least, distracted him from his discomfort. She carried on, and David began to calm himself. His struggling subsided.

The nurse's head snapped up from his charting, and he concentrated intently on the heart monitor. Mother didn't process the severe spiking of the graph on the monitor above them. She did, however, see the urgency in the RN's movements as he shoved himself back from the table and strode quickly to David's bedside. She had already pushed her chair out to the side to allow easy access.

The nurse leaned over David, and listened to his heart with his stethoscope. He looked puzzled, and remarked on the strange results. Without further comment, he returned to the charting table, his back to the group and his eyes on the monitor.

Mother resumed her chest pounding when David became more agitated. Once again, he started to settle. And, again, the nurse's head jolted up to look at the angry line spiking heavily across the screen. Mother moved out of the way as she had before, and David looked up in agitation at the nurse.

After checking his patient and discovering nothing new, the nurse asked, "Has he had problems with his heart?"

"No," Mother replied, "it's more a breathing thing with him. He was born at twenty-four weeks gestation, so his lungs were compromised at birth. He has a chronic lung condition, so he gets chest infections easily."

As the nurse checked David's IV, a group of physicians approached his bedside. They asked the usual questions and examined him. The confirmed diagnosis was pneumonia, a dangerous infection for compromised lungs. As usual, there wasn't a bed available in pediatrics, so he would have to stay in the emergency department until one became vacant. With more stability, he would be moved out of the trauma unit, and placed in a regular emergency room, or in the hallway, to wait for a bed. Mother and Luke would have to make themselves comfortable in chairs, and doze off between routine checks, until he moved to the pediatrics floor, which could be anywhere from a few hours to a number of days.

At six o'clock in the morning, Mother unfolded herself from the rigid armchair and the thick, woven blanket she had wrapped herself in. She stretched her cramped muscles and massaged the kink in her neck.

Luke emerged from his twisted sleeping position, his awkward movements more from disorientation than sore muscles. "I'm tired," he said, moving toward the garish, flower-patterned curtain that closed the room off from the bustle of the department. "I have to pee."

Mother escorted him to the bathroom. While she waited, a porter went into David's room, carrying a chart the size and depth of an ancient Webster dictionary. The label on it said "Thinned Chart." The porter placed the heavy document near David's feet, then began making preparations to move him upstairs to the pediatrics floor.

She and Luke were soon following behind the porter as she pushed the stretcher, equipped with an IV pole, an oxygen tank, and David, toward the elevator that would take them upstairs. They emerged into an open foyer on the fourth floor, and moved toward the automatic doors that slid open to greet them. They had always reminded Mother of the sliding doors from *Star Trek*. The concept was considered science fiction at the time. The only thing missing was the familiar "schlick" sound as the Starship *Enterprise* doors opened or closed.

As they made their way down the hallway, they came to the bridge suspended over the courtyard four floors below. The bridge connected to the other side of the pediatrics unit, and the space above the bridge was made to look like a jungle scene with a T-Rex's upper body intruding from the background foliage. Luke and Mother walked under the display without much notice. David, lying on his back on the stretcher, took in a different perspective. He was never sure if he should be frightened or excited.

The sign that greeted them above the door said "Stollery Children's Hospital."

"Welcome to Hogwarts," muttered Luke, as they passed over the threshold.

A friendly nurse directed them to the room where David would stay. There was only one bed in the room, since he would be quarantined until the pneumonia was under control. The staff skillfully moved David onto the stretcher with the aid of a sliding board, then positioned him in his bed. The oxygen tubing was removed from the accompanying portable tank and attached to the wall. His IV bag, containing a salt-water solution, was moved from the pole attached to his stretcher to a standing pole by the bedside, and the height adjusted. The tubing from the bag on the pole was then run through a machine that monitored the number of drops of fluid that coursed down the tube into his vein. A large red, plastic container with thick tubing protruded from the wall. Its purpose was to suction excess phlegm from his mouth and throat whenever necessary. His catheter bag was hung from a slot in the underframe of the bed: his intake and output of fluids frequently recorded. Another machine, which monitored his temperature and heart rate, was set up by attaching leads to small pads stuck to his chest, arms, and legs. A cuff was adjusted around his upper arm to monitor his blood pressure. A nurse placed a type of press, not unlike a clothes pin, over David's finger to monitor the amount of oxygen in his blood. If the numbers were too low, the amount of oxygen coming through the mask was increased to keep him from turning a dusky blue around his eyes and mouth.

All of these machines and tubes, as intrusive and overwhelming as they looked, brought Mother comfort, peace of mind, and hope. For her, this routine was as commonplace as lining up in Costco on a Saturday afternoon.

Chapter 24
Mending

Mother unzipped the backpack she had brought with her, and removed toiletry items to place at David's bedside. She pulled out a small tape recorder, music tapes, three stuffed animals, and two books.

Luke had parked himself in a chair by the window overlooking the courtyard. Under the glass on the court side, lush, green plants spilled over the side of a window box. Beneath every ledge, on all five floors of the hospital, window boxes offered a spectacular sight for those looking up from below. From where he sat, he could see the mosaic cobblestone pattern of the enormous foyer, and the few corralled trees that seemed to have sprung from the earth through the floor. There was a seating area for patrons who purchased drinks and food from the different vendors located on the main floor. He scanned the crowd for any staff members or patients he knew.

To one side, a waterfall cascaded down a rock face, spreading into a clear pool decorated with pink lotus blossoms. The pond shone with the reflection of hundreds of coins contributed in hopes of fulfilling a wish. Directly across from where he looked out the window was a pair of glass elevators, which moved visitors and patients from floor to floor. His attention was drawn to one man, who attempted to discreetly readjust the crotch of his trousers by turning his back on the other people in the elevator. This tactic only exposed him to the possibility of five floors of voyeuristic eyes. When the man looked up toward Luke, he appeared to be looking past him. Behind Luke lay David, who had kicked off his covers, twisted his hospital gown up around his chest, and was kicking furiously to free himself. Luke pulled the curtain around to one side of the bed to give David privacy from onlookers in the glass elevator. It was like living in a goldfish bowl.

"David's in trouble," Luke said, nonchalantly.

Mother returned from the hallway with an armful of fresh linen, wash cloths, towels, extra diapers, lotion, and a pair of red-striped pajamas. She placed it all on the wide ledge of the windowsill to ensure she was prepared for the morning, in case there was a shortage of anything. She started to remove David's gown and replaced the awkward garment with the pajamas.

Luke looked at them admiringly. "So cool, David."

"If you like the look of prison stripes," Mother said jokingly.

David let out a noisy cough, and Mother reached for the suction tubing to remove the secretions from his mouth. She pulled the stethoscope off the top of the IV pole and listened to his breathing sounds. A quick glance at the monitor showed no changes as David started to fret again. Automatically, she cupped her hand and started pounding on the upper left side of his chest in an effort to loosen secretions trapped in his lungs.

Luke's ears perked up when he heard the whistle. Dr. Liam stopped at the sink to wash his hands before moving to David's bedside; an entourage of residents followed. His tie had Dr. Seuss's Cat in the Hat boldly displayed on it.

After a quick greeting, they discussed David's condition and his diagnosis of pneumonia. "Has David ever had an issue with his heart?" Dr. Liam asked.

"No."

"I didn't think so. But there was some concern in ER. Cardiology was consulted."

David became agitated again, and Mother resumed the chest pounding.

Dr. Liam chatted to the residents before he looked at the monitor over David's bed. The lines had changed to a severely spiked, but rhythmic, pattern. He moved nearer to Mother and continued to watch the monitor, before gently placing his hand on her forearm. "Stop," he said.

The spiking line dropped to one that coursed across the screen in shallow dips.

Dr. Liam smiled, and turned to one of his residents. "Call cardiology and cancel the referral. I think we found our cause."

He laughed before speaking to Mother again. "Were you pounding on his chest in ER when they had him on the leads?"

Mother shrugged. "Probably. The pounding settles him—it puts him to sleep."

"Don't do that," he said. "You had everybody in a panic in the ER, thinking he was having a heart attack. Every time you pounded on his chest, the impact was recorded on the screen and it looked like his heart was out of control. We couldn't figure out why it was so inconsistent."

"But I pound on his chest all the time. Why wasn't this caught before?"

"The nurse probably didn't see what you were doing and didn't make the connection."

Dr. Liam bent over David and planted a kiss on his forehead. "Keep your Mother out of trouble." His words were met with a smile. He gave Luke a quick squeeze. "Continue to keep your Mother and brother entertained." Then he looked at Mother. "You're here for at least ten days. We'll keep an eye on his oxygen needs, and once that stabilizes, you can go home. We'll keep him in isolation for now."

Mother's eyes became moist with tears, partly from relief that his condition wasn't more serious, and partly because hospital stays were so exhausting.

Dr. Liam opened his arms wide. "I think somebody needs a hug," he said.

Mother engaged in the quick embrace, which was all she needed to ground herself. She took in a ragged breath.

"See you this evening," Dr. Liam said as he made his way toward the door. His residents shuffled behind him in close pursuit, clustering around him as he stopped at the sink to wash his hands before exiting the room.

Chapter 25
Diagnosing

Dr. Liam gathered his residents to discuss David's condition in more detail, so they could be questioned on premature births and what they had noticed about David's physical condition. A nurse dressed in a printed blue smock and white pants passed by with a cardboard tray holding three cups of coffee, heading for the nurse's station. She nodded and smiled at Dr. Liam.

"One of those mine?" he asked.

The nurse stopped and looked over her tray, a crooked smile spreading across her face. "Maybe."

"I was only kidding," he said.

"No, actually there's an extra here. You take it black, right?" she asked, handing him a cup.

"Thanks, Dora," he said appreciatively. "Where are the donuts?"

"Right beside my raise," she replied, and continued on her way to the station.

Dr. Liam, sipping his coffee, returned to the conversation with his residents. He pressed them for answers, had them question their own responses, and queried other notions. As they continued their discussion, a harried looking middle-aged man approached them.

"Bill!" Dr. Liam called out.

The man stopped and faced the group. His leather jacket was unzipped, and his shirt was adorned with a Superman tie.

"How's Katie?" Dr. Liam asked.

"No real change," Bill replied.

"Hmm. What do you think's going on?"

"I feel certain there's something happening with her gut, just by the way she's acting. It's happened before."

"We should consult medicine, then?"

"I think so. Something is making fast work of itself. Her temp is not going down and she isn't as responsive. She's worse than she was last night."

"Ok. I'll set something up with GI."

"Thanks," Bill said. He placed a hand on Dr. Liam's shoulder before he moved on.

One of the residents watched as Bill turned the corner. "Is he a pediatric specialist?"

"No, no. I actually think he's an accountant for the TD bank. He's Katie's father," Dr. Liam said.

He took another sip of his coffee. "Kids with severe disabilities can be tricky, and you're going to run into some difficult cases that will baffle you. These kids don't follow any rules. Don't expect certain signs to indicate something specific just because you think they should. You're going to try everything you can think of, pull out all the knowledge you've gained in your studies and all the knowledge you can draw from other specialists...but it won't be enough. If there's only one thing you remember my telling you, let it be this. When you're uncertain about what to do in difficult circumstances—and before you've failed at everything else—ask the parents. They're the specialists. The parents are the ones who have spent countless hours and years researching everything they can find out about their child's condition. They spend all their time with their child and know how their child reacts, what works and what doesn't. Spend more time asking than telling, because these parents are the experts, not you."

He stopped for a moment, as if in serious thought, then said, "Now let's go check on our Katie."

The flock turned and ambled down the hall to another room. Dr. Liam began whistling a tune to cue the family of his arrival. He tossed his empty coffee cup into a bin by the door before going inside to wash his hands at the sink.

Chapter 26
Awakening

~~~~~~~

It had been five days since David's admission to hospital. He had been moved from a private room to a semi-private room. He was not cured, but had improved to a point where he no longer required isolation. He had been placed in a double room to free the isolation room for another patient who needed it.

Before breakfast, Mother was roused by the sound of a whimpering child being brought into their room. She rose from the cot that she and Luke had slept on, and pulled the curtain around them to give the newcomers privacy. She heard the nurses discussing the child with a family member in English, gathering information essential for the chart. Comforting sounds in a different language from a soft female voice floated through the air, but the child's responses were in a universal language—the sound of fear. Another woman's voice added to the chorus, and she too provided soothing sounds, repeating the name, Kareem Mohammad Aaban, which sounded as soft as velvet over the crying sounds of the small child.

Mother overheard some of the medical history, and thought she caught the term *nephrotic*, which meant a kidney problem. Once the child began to settle down and the nursing staff had left, she checked on David to see if he was awake. It was time to get ready before doctors' rounds anyway.

Luke had rolled over and wrapped himself up like a burrito in the wheat-coloured blanket, his bare feet protruding from the bottom. The sound of his breathing showed that nothing had interfered with his slumber.

Mother called David's name softly, to waken him slowly and begin his morning routine. She marveled at how he woke up, a ritual that never began with his eyes. At the moment of waking, he smiled, as if a new day was always something to feel excited about. His cheeks glowed at the sound of his name. His arms reached upwards, his back arched, and his legs extended into a full body stretch, kick-starting his circulation and igniting his spirit. His smile stretched further across his face to display gleaming white teeth—the prelude to a faint flutter of long, dark eyelashes. Sea-green eyes sparkled with life, and glowed with love.

"Hhhhi." This was always the first sound he uttered before Mother placed a kiss on his cheek in the greeting of a brand-new day.

The nurses' days were busy, so parents of children on the pediatric wards tended to most of the daily care, in an effort to be helpful. Mother began by filling a basin with warm water and giving David a sponge bath, then drying each limb and body part. She put his joints through a range of limbering motions. Afterwards, she slathered his skin with body butter that smelled like coconuts and gave his muscles a deep massage, rubbing the areas that revealed degrees of redness due to pressure. She swished his toothbrush in water before scrubbing his teeth. Toothpaste was avoided, since he was unable to spit and the substance could disturb his stomach if swallowed on a regular basis. After drying his hair with a rough towel, she combed out his curls with a bit of gel to tame them.

She started to change his diaper, and he pumped his legs in fun to make it more difficult for her to lift him and slide the diaper underneath. When it was fastened, she unfolded a pair of flannel pajamas, already made cozy by the blanket heater. With his help, she pulled on the pajama top, threading his arms through the holes and counting the buttons as she did them up. They made it into a game, with David vocalizing after the enunciation of each number. She pulled up his pajama pants and moved him from side to side, sliding them all the way up and snapping the loose waistband against his middle, making him laugh.

After the bathing and dressing exercise, Mother slid him to the side of the mattress and, watching the tension on his IV line, lifted him and placed him in his chair. She buckled, snapped, and velcroed him in, then began changing the bedsheets. She would flutter a sheet and catch him up in it, slowly dragging it off his smiling face before repeating the process. The peek-a-boo game had become a favourite amusement, earning him the nickname "Boo."

With fresh sheets on the bed, she lifted him onto it, positioning him on his back. She arranged pillows to sufficiently support him, and looked in the cup attached to the line running from the wall. Earlier in the morning, the nurse had provided the syringes of medication for Mother to administer into his G-tube. She had also left a pool of Ventolin in the bottom of the plastic cup. Mother rigged it up with a mask, then placed it over her son's face, turning up the oxygen level to make the liquid mist. She encouraged him to take in long, slow breaths. As he did so, she pulled out a book from the shelf above his head, and opened it to the page marker halfway through. The story of wizards and magic had become very popular. She found enjoyment in the reading for both David and herself. He was intrigued by the character named Hagrid, and loved it when Mother tried to imitate his gruff speech and accent. She kept one hand on the mask to keep it centred on his face as he breathed in the cool, cloud-like mist. The Ventolin treatment would need to be repeated three to four times more before David's bedtime.

She read until his treatment was completed, then lay him flat, reclining his position until his head was lower than his feet. Then she began pounding on his chest in the ongoing attempt to break up phlegm collected in his lungs. The rhythm and shaking of his body at every beat often lulled him to sleep. After a while, the rhythm of his breathing was matched with Luke's.

After twenty minutes of pounding each front and back quarter of David's upper body, she propped him up in bed and tickled the inside of his hands, a gesture that made him laugh and cough up secretions that had moved higher in his chest. She grabbed the suction tubing that extended from the wall and positioned the wand in his mouth.

She snapped open a few of the cans of formula, turned the liquid over into a plastic formula bag, and hung it on the top of a specific pole. It was different from the homemade device she had fashioned to make it easier for Luke to turn the cans over into a metal funnel. Calculations for the number of drops to be administered were already set into the machine that clutched the tubing, and she hit the start button, making sure the machine would not ring due to occlusions or a kinking in the tube. She pulled out the book again. An eager smile spread across David's face, and she began to read—quietly, to lessen the amount of disruption to others in the room. As she read, there were sounds of stirring from the other side of the room, as two women spoke softly in a language foreign to her ears.

Luke woke up, and emerged like a new butterfly from his blanket cocoon. He rubbed the sleep from his eyes and breathed a long sigh. Mother helped get him off the cot and out behind the curtain to the bathroom for his own morning routine. As he closed the bathroom door, a whistle sounded in the hallway. Mother went back to David and waited for Dr. Liam and his entourage to fill the space, surrounding her son like a liquid, symbolizing his ability and will to stay afloat.

When the medical consultation was over, and there was agreement that David would need a few more days to meet his oxygen requirements for dismissal, the group dispersed, leaving Dr. Liam sitting on the cot by David's bed. Luke had returned, and now had a seat in the middle of Dr. Liam's lap, his body leaning against the physician.

"You'll be here again this evening to check on us?" Mother asked. The connection to Dr. Liam was crucial, and she felt safe as long as she could rely on his attention to David. Something serious could happen that would suddenly threaten his life. It wasn't fair that so much responsibility was placed on one man, but he had a gift for recognizing problems other physicians missed, and dismissed assumptions made by others who did not connect to these children in the same way. Rightly or wrongly, she felt certain that he remained their major link to survival—a link shared by countless other families with severely disabled children.

Dr. Liam did not loosen his grip on Luke, nor did he shift his eyes in Mother's direction when he spoke. "I have a funeral to attend to this afternoon. It's the Carpenter family...Cathy...and I'm giving the eulogy. You may know of her. She was in here a lot." He looked at the floor. "This is the second funeral my staff and I have attended in the past three weeks. It's been a pretty rough month," he said with a slight break in his voice.

"I guess that's what happens when you deal with such delicate kids," Mother replied. "You've got to remember that you give them a longer life than they would have had."

He shrugged. "I don't know about that." He eased Luke off of his lap, and stood to go. "I'll be back this evening, but it might be a little later than usual. Keep this guy breathing and happy." He slapped his hand down on David's blanketed leg and gave it a shake. David's eyes popped open at the abruptness of the move, then he flashed a crooked smile.

"I think somebody needs a hug," said Luke. He threw his arms around the physician's waist.

"That I do, Luke," Dr. Liam said gently, returning the embrace. He left the room and headed for his next patient.

Mother turned to her sons. "Let's get ourselves organized. I need to get to class before I get sacked. Auntie June will be here in about a half an hour to watch over you two for the morning. I'll be back later this afternoon."

Luke pulled a T-shirt over his head. "Can I take David for a walk around the hospital today?" The question got an excited squeal in response.

"You'll have to check with the nurses and Auntie June. If it's OK with them, you have to promise me you won't get into any trouble."

Luke scoffed. "How could we get into any trouble in here?"

She opened her eyes wide in surprise, and felt certain she had caught a glimpse of the boys exchanging smiles. Mother tried to think positive, hoping at the same time that whatever happened, the damage wouldn't be permanent. She looked through her bag for clean clothes to change into, then disappeared into the bathroom to get ready for school.

Chapter 27
Disappearing

Auntie June arrived later than usual in the morning. Although she was not a large person, there was little space for her in the room, now filled with a number of other bodies on the opposite side of the room. By ten o'clock at least eight women and two older men were holding a vigil for a young boy in the other bed. As each new group of people arrived, bags filled with personal treasures, such as toys, books, games, and a variety of food, accompanied them. Everything was laid out on the counter or the bedside table, or on the bed. A faint smell of bread, spices, and ripe fruit hung in the air. The older men sat on the bed with the boy, and the women pulled chairs nearer. They straightened their intricately decorated suits (long tunics over loosely fitting pants) and repositioned the scarves that lay across their collar bones and hung down their backs. One of the women, approached June and apologized for any intrusion, respectfully offering to take everyone outside in the foyer to allow for privacy.

June explained it was time for David to get up and moving anyway, and that she had requested that the nurses move him into the chair so they could go for a walk. Besides, it would be good to allow the other family some time to themselves. When they returned, though, it would be nice to give him a rest. The woman named Shaista agreed.

Three nurses helped lift David into his chair, remarking on how such a small being could be so heavy. He enjoyed the attention, and moved his legs impatiently, making the process of strapping him in more difficult. But the group eventually made their way off the unit, after first wrestling with an awkward door. They took the glass elevator to the main floor, and peeked into the shops in the foyer. Auntie June discovered a stuffed hedgehog that David admired. She purchased it for him along with a small bag of large marbles for Luke. The ritual of buying David a stuffed animal for every hospital admission or surgical procedure had started from the time of his birth. He had acquired twenty-five stuffed-animal friends. Today's addition made it twenty-six.

"Let's call him Spike," Luke said. David smiled in agreement.

They continued on their way, stopping at the different tables that sold bracelets, purses, nuts, candy, books, and trinkets. Around the corner and further away from the glass elevators was another set of elevators, which were primarily for staff and hospital carts. The visitor traffic wasn't as heavy here. June fell into a panic at the discovery that her clutch purse was missing, and wanted to return to the shop where they had purchased Spike. The hallways had become more crowded now with patients, staff, and visitors, and she did not relish the idea of pushing the boys back to the place where she had bought the newest addition to the stuffed menagerie.

"We could go upstairs and wait for you. We get off at Level 4, right?" Luke asked in an attempt to help.

David moved eagerly in his chair at the prospect of a ride. He loved elevators.

"OK," June said, glancing up at the numbers above the elevator cars, which seemed to take forever to move. "I'll be quick and meet you upstairs right outside these elevators. I'll take the glass one's up and meet you outside the service ones. OK?" She hurried off.

The boys stood outside the elevator, waiting for the sound to indicate the arrival of the car. When the doors opened, Luke triumphantly pushed David in, then spun him around so that he could face out. Then Luke leaned forward and hit all the buttons on the pad, to prolong their journey and offer David a better ride. As he bent forward, one of his newly acquired marbles slipped from his pocket, hit the hard floor, and bounced out onto the linoleum flooring outside the elevator. He jumped out after it, and as he got closer, his foot accidentally kicked it a few more feet. He ran after it again. At last, he scooped up the marble in his fist and turned, victorious, with the small sphere clutched tightly in his fist, just in time to see David's smiling face disappear behind the heavy doors. He heard an excited, high-pitched squeal from behind the massive wall.

"Damn it!" Luke said aloud to no one. "All the buttons are pushed so it'll take forever to get to the top!"

He ran down the corridor to the nearby stairwell, sidestepping others and excusing himself to get around the visitors. He hit the stairway, and sprinted up to the next floor. He ran down the hallway, and skidded around the corner in front of the service elevators. He was too late to rescue David, but was just in time to see the doors sliding closed, once again hiding his brother's smiling face and excited shriek. He slammed his hand on the button but was too slow, and heard the elevator advancing to the next floor before he took off down the corridor towards the stairs again.

He took two stairs at a time, pulling himself upwards more quickly by use of the side rail. At the next landing, he threw open the door and slid around the corner into the hallway and toward the public glass elevators. Through the glass on the left side of the metal doors, he could see his aunt's profile. The elevator doors opened to discharge those who wished to exit. His aunt had two more floors to go. He threw his jacket hood over his head and squatted down beside a stretcher being pushed by an attendant, walking alongside it, shielding himself from his aunt's sight.

At the intersecting corridors to the service elevators, he ran. He spun around in front of them as the doors closed. Again, he could hear David's faint laughter coming from the other side. He took off once more, racing up the steps to the next floor, running full-tilt to get to the elevators at the same time as his brother. He careened around the corner for his last chance to retrieve his sibling before getting to the fourth floor where June would meet them. He had beaten the elevator this time—the doors were shut! But the illuminated numbers were retreating. He had missed it. His body went cold, and an edge of panic set in. A few of the staff talked among themselves outside the elevators. One, wearing a security-guard uniform, carried a walkie-talkie in his hand. A string of keys was tethered to his belt loop.

He interrupted their conversation, asking in a shrill voice if there had been a boy in a wheelchair on the elevator. The guard said there was, and that the button had been pressed for the fifth floor, but no one was with the boy. He had turned the button off with his key and sent the car back down to the main floor, where another security guard would collect him and take him to admitting to find out where he belonged. Luke took off toward the stairs, his open jacket flapping behind him like a Batman cloak.

His feet barely touched the steps as he slid his way back down the stairs. He encountered a housekeeping staffer halfway down mopping the floor. Gingerly stepping past her, he expressed his apologies each time his sneaker left a print on the freshly washed steps. He picked up speed again, made it to the bottom floor, and sped out the door toward the service elevators. As he rounded the corner to his destination, he saw a security guard. He was holding David's wrist, to get a good look at his hospital identification band and figure out who he was and where he came from.

Luke threw up his hands in exasperation and relief. "Oh, wow!" He dropped to one knee in front of his brother. "Thank you for finding him, sir. Our mother is waiting for us upstairs. Darndest thing how that elevator took off without me and my mom."

David squealed in delight at the sight of his brother, and pumped his legs up and down inside his straps.

"I'll just get him back upstairs, pronto," Luke said as he reached past and pushed the elevator button to go back up.

"Not so fast," the security guard said. He pulled himself up to his full height and eyed Luke suspiciously. He pulled his walkie-talkie out of his pocket.

"OK, fine. The truth is I lost him. It wasn't on purpose."

The guard listened attentively as Luke related his story.

On the fourth floor, June stood outside the service elevators waiting for the boys. She glanced down the hall to see if they might be standing by the large saltwater fish tank outside ICU. She considered returning to the room to see if they had grown impatient and gone directly there. Then a bell sounded and the elevator door opened, revealing both boys and a security guard.

She addressed the boys with a mildly concerned voice. "Are you two all right?"

"Um...well...," Luke said uncertainly, shifting his eyes toward the guard.

"The boys are fine," the guard replied. "They had a little adventure with the elevator, but all seems well. I think I'll escort you all to the bridge to make sure you get across."

June had no idea what he was talking about. "Thank you for your help," she said, looking at David. "I should get this one back to his room and into bed. He's been up long enough and must be tired."

"I'd say that if anyone is tired, it would have to be the other one."

June offered no response. As they walked across the bridge toward the unit, Luke asked, "Are you going to tell Mom?"

"You haven't told me what happened yet," June said. "And don't start with 'it wasn't my fault.' Fault doesn't matter—just tell me what happened. And remember, the Creator was watching."

Luke looked up warily. He wasn't sure what he was looking for, but he thought it was about to drop on his head.

"OK, tell me the story," June said.

He explained with neither embellishment nor self-defense. "I didn't mean for it to happen."

"Well, I didn't expect it to happen either," June said. "But you found him, Luke. Everything is fine."

"Are you going to tell Mom?"

"Probably. But remember that you eventually took responsibility in your heart for your actions. Doing something takes more than just the physicality of it, which, by the way, is why your mother is so exhausted all the time."

"So she's not actually crazy?"

"She's overwhelmed, more than anything else. And I *do* have to tell her. But on the bright side, this has a happy ending. You told the truth and took responsibility. That's what it's about, Luke."

As they neared David's room, the hum of voices grew louder. The room was still crowded with visitors. Like a small prince, the young boy sat cross-legged in the middle of the bedspread. His short, black hair was neatly trimmed around his ears. Instead of his pajamas being striped like David's, they were made of midnight-blue silk, embroidered along the edges with gold thread. He held an action figure in his hands. As June, Luke, and David entered, he pointed a finger directly at David. "Momma," he asked innocently, "what is the matter with that boy?"

Mother entered in time to hear the words, which had been spoken a thousand times in David's presence. She dropped her heavy backpack onto a chair and pulled off her jacket.

"Shhh, that's not nice," the boy's mother said, holding a finger to her lips.

Chapter 28
Explaining

~~~~~~

Mother felt the tension within the room. "Best get you into bed, Boo," she said.

She undid the succession of straps that held David in his chair, and pulled off the brakes to unlock the wheels. She checked the IV lines to make sure they were slack and would not pull when she lifted him. She squatted with a straight back, slid one arm under his knees and the other behind his head, curling it under his left arm, and grasped his wrist. She raised her elbow to catch the back of his neck, since he could not hold his head up on his own. With a graceful, sweeping motion, she lifted him into the air, pushing up with her legs, holding him solidly against her. Kicking the wheelchair out of her way, she stepped forward and deposited him safely and softly on the bed. She took a few of his stuffed toys from the window shelf and placed them strategically around him to support limbs and tubes. She stood back and looked at her own little prince, his crown of golden hair set against the starched whiteness of the pillowcase. He was like a hero from a beloved children's story, surrounded by an army of deeply loved animal helpers.

Luke concentrated on the other boy. He approached their roommate with curiosity, fascinated by his darker skin. Luke went to school with Chinese, African, and Spanish children, but this boy looked different. He was also intrigued by the type of dress the women wore and the smell of the strange food.

He stopped at the end of the boy's bed. "My name is Luke. His name is David, and he has cerebral palsy. He was born with it and it won't ever go away. He can't walk or talk, but he can understand what you say. To understand him, you have to look at his face, sort of like you do with babies."

The boy nodded in understanding. His large extended family came with an assortment of new babies. "Does he go to school?" he asked.

Luke grinned and turned to his brother. "David, do you go to school?"

David's head moved and a smile flooded his face.

"Ah, that would be a yes," Kareem responded.

"Absolutely! He loves school."

Luke's eyes fell on a remaining dish of food sitting on the bed-tray table. There was also a plate of what looked like huge potato chips on it.

"What is that?" he asked, pointing at the traditional bread.

"It is called a papadum," said Kareem.

Kareem's mother picked up the plate and, as she did so, a succession of bright red and gold bracelets slid down her arm to her wrist, making a jangling sound.

She held out the plate to Luke. "It is a crisp bread, and it breaks easily. It's also one of Kareem's favourites."

Luke reached out tentatively.

"Break a little off," Kareem said. He demonstrated with a piece of his own.

Luke broke off a shard and put the piece into his mouth. "That's pretty good!"

"What little curry we have left is now cold. Tomorrow, I can bring you hot food. Do you like vegetables and rice?" asked Kareem's mother.

"Yes, I do," replied Luke.

"You don't need to bother with that," Mother said politely. "I'm sure you have lots to do without cooking for us."

"It is no bother. Besides," the other woman said as she swept her hand across the room. "I have lots of help."

"Then we would love it," Mother said gratefully. She couldn't remember the last time she had enjoyed a curry or a samosa, but she recalled their delicious taste.

"Kareem, let us all go out to the playroom and see what they have there for you to do. I will get you ready," his mother said.

Mother pulled the curtain around their space and sat beside David, now snuggled into his bed. June returned with fresh coffee, and pulled up a chair on the other side. Luke sat in her lap.

Mother caught June's eye and pointed to the group on the other side of the curtain. As they noisily exited the room, she silently mouthed, "Crowded."

June smiled and returned the silent exchange. "Family."

Mother sat back, and retreated into her thoughts. She suddenly felt terribly alone, until she looked up at June and was filled with a comforting warmth.

"Attach yourself to them," June said softly. "Pull from their energy and strength of community."

Mother nodded. She felt a lump in her throat, but swallowed and turned her attention to her backpack. "I have some reading to do by tomorrow. Who wants to hear Act 1 of *The Merchant of Venice?*"

Luke stuck out his tongue, but David offered a warm smile.

"You'll listen to anything, won't you?" she said with affection.

She was never certain if he understood what she read to him, or if he simply loved the sound of a voice. Either way, she read to him daily: picture books, novels, plays, brochures, newspapers, whatever print she had access to. Her voice relaxed him and allowed him to sleep for a while without the need for drugs. Luke preferred more choice of what he listened to, and the content had to hold his attention.

"If you have to read, then read this," Luke said, handing her *Harry Potter*.

A knock on the door was followed by an inquisitive voice. "Hello?"

Mother pulled back the curtain. The room was now empty of the other family, but the luscious scent of spicy food lingered. Beth stood in the doorway, looking worn out.

"Oh, no!" Mother said with concern. "Is it Chris?"

"Yes, we're across the hall." Beth hesitated, then said, "When you have a minute, could you come over just to talk?"

Mother looked back at June, who waved her away. "Go ahead. I'll stay with the boys for a little longer."

Mother gave her the book she had in her hand and followed Beth out of the room.

June lifted the book and waved it at the boys. "Now, where were you the last time?"

Luke shrugged his shoulders. "I think somebody just died."

"I think that happens a lot in this book," she said. "Death is a mysterious part of life."

Luke looked at her curiously, then out toward the room across the hall. He felt a hard knot grip his stomach in a way he did not understand. He still felt guilty about the horrible thing he had said about his brother.

Chapter 29
Coping

Mother followed Beth down the corridor and into a large room with six beds. Chris was next to the window, and he gave her a big grin as she came to his bedside. She recognized most of the women and children who were also gathered there. There was one new addition—a woman she had seen in Dr. Liam's office a few times. She remembered hearing that she worked in a clothing store. The woman's daughter was in her late teens, but Dr. Liam's philosophy was that he would continue to see his patients regardless of their ages until they expired, or he did, whichever came first.

The retail worker was introduced as Rhonda. The other women stood protectively around her as she sat slumped in a chair at the end of a bed, shredding a soggy tissue. Mother found a full Kleenex box and passed it to her, then glanced at Beth. "How is Chris?"

Beth waved her hand. "Fine. Minor setback. We should be out of here in a few days." Her eyes returned to Rhonda. "Livia is in ICU."

Mother looked at Rhonda, who appeared fragile enough for a loud noise or harsh word to shatter her. "What happened?" Mother asked as she pulled up a nearby footstool.

Rhonda took a deep breath. "What happened? Livia got older, is what happened. For starters, she was bigger, heavier to lift, and more awkward to move when she turned seventeen, and had developed scoliosis. Like your son, she has a severe form of cerebral palsy and needs complete support. I'm a single parent, I have to work, and getting a caregiver on a regular basis for her before and after school was a nightmare. If an agency sent someone, they didn't last. Liv was too much work and too great a responsibility for the wage they get. At that point, I had little choice but to contact Rosewood, a respite institution, and ask for help."

Mother knew the care at Rosewood was exemplary. David went there on occasional weekends for respite care, but the facility was in high demand and minimally funded. As good as it was, she understood how horrible it would feel to see it as a last resort if you really wanted your child at home.

"The administrator said they could take her, but she could only stay in the care home until she was eighteen and then had to be moved. I didn't know what that would involve. This change turned out to be the beginning of hell. First of all, having her taken from my home when I wasn't ready for it was like experiencing her death. I mourned the transition for a long time."

The women listened, and Mother took in the movements around her. Barbara, a young mother who probably wasn't much more than twenty, poured a glass of water from a pitcher and passed it to Rhonda, who absentmindedly accepted it. Daniel, Barbara's three-year-old son, sat in a stroller next to her. She reached down to give him a reassuring pat. He was a tiny child with a debilitating disorder. His red hair stood straight up like *Charlie Brown*'s Woodstock. He did not speak, but when he was startled or needed something, he shivered and made a peeping sound. His hand was caught on the inside of a strap, and Barbara released it, pulling his stroller closer to her.

Rhonda carried on with her story. "Regardless of how hard the separation was on me, Livia did well at Rosewood, and I took her home on weekends for quality time together. But when she turned eighteen, she wasn't entitled to a placement there any longer. They had no choice but to turn her out. As a result, she was put into a long-term care facility until they could find a group home for her. It wasn't an easy stay."

She explained that the care Livia received in the new facility wasn't the same as she would have had at home. Answers to complaints about questionable care were always the same: "We are short-staffed and doing the best we can."

"The night came when I got a phone call to say that Livia was in respiratory distress, and the ambulance had been called. I put my coat over my pajamas and headed for the hospital, only to learn that the ambulance had been routed to a different one because it was too full. They have no idea what problems that policy causes. I was in panic mode. Livia was now in a facility where no one knew her and Dr. Liam had no access. I felt nothing but dread."

Rhonda went on to explain that when she arrived at the Tamarine hospital, she desperately tried to have Livia transferred back to the South Side hospital and Dr. Liam. Although she was told it was possible, it became evident that it was not.

"Livia was put on an adult medical floor. Although everyone was kind and concerned, things went from bad to worse because they did not understand her. Medicine floors rotate their doctors frequently, and the treatment plan wasn't what I felt would benefit her either, but my concerns fell on deaf ears. Her feeds were cut back to stop her from aspirating, and she became weak. In time, her condition worsened. She began to react in pain whenever her leg was touched, and a reddened area appeared on her thigh. Attempts to get the wound team to examine it were refused, since it didn't appear severe enough. After several weeks, she was discharged, but she wasn't herself."

Rhonda's story was interrupted by a cry in the ward, and all six mothers' heads swiveled toward the sound. Brian, a small two-year-old Hispanic child with warm brown eyes fringed with thick, dark lashes, had little to no independent movement and suffered from frequent indigestion. His foster mother, Ana, also Hispanic, tenderly scooped him up from the bed, minding his lines and tubes, and held him comfortably in her lap. She cuddled him close to her chest, rocking him, and softly hummed a lullaby until his cry subsided. She guided his hand to his mouth and held it there so he could suck his thumb. He settled down quickly.

"She was only out for a brief period of time before she became sick again and was returned to the South Side hospital. She had a long drawn-out ordeal in ICU, and then went onto a medical floor. Although Dr. Liam was not the attending physician, he was consulted, which meant he could visit. After Doc Liam examined her, he discovered that the reddened area on her leg was actually a deep wound that went down to the bone. They had to take the softened, top skin off to expose it. The affected area was the size of a grapefruit when they opened it up. The wound team is trying its best to repair the damage, but it is slow going. She doesn't have the strength to heal it anymore."

"Where is she now?" asked Ana.

Rhonda lifted her head, trying to choke back sobs. "She's back in ICU. She's having trouble breathing again, so she's been intubated once more. They are planning to send her back to this floor because they don't think they can do much more, and Dr. Liam was able to get her on pediatrics."

"Oh, Rhonda. Who is here with you?" asked Ana.

Rhonda shook her head. "No one. People are so busy."

"We are with you," Beth said. "You're not alone."

* * *

June was almost finished reading a chapter in the *Harry Potter* book. David appeared sleepy, but Luke had his eyes glued to the page, reading silently along as best as he could. The room was quiet: she suspected the other boy and his family had gone out again. She had not heard a sound from them over the course of the last few chapters. After the last sentence, she snapped the book shut and rose to stretch. "Are you two enjoying the book?" she asked as she reached for the bedside curtain.

David grinned widely, and Luke nodded enthusiastically. "Yes, it's very good," he said.

"I think so too." She drew aside the curtain, and was greeted by a sight that surprised and amused her. Kareem and his family sat together on the bed, on chairs, or in laps, all facing David's curtain in captivated attention. They broke into polite applause and big smiles.

"We will continue with the reading tomorrow," June said with a laugh.

"Same time, same station," Luke added.

Their broad smiles lightened the atmosphere, until they saw Mother approaching, looking drained and exhausted. June wasn't certain how to read her demeanor, but it appeared she was carrying the burden of some rather bad news.

Chapter 30
Enlightening

Mother grabbed her heavy book bag from the chair and slid it to the floor. There was still homework to do, and she looked at it helplessly. June touched her arm, and Mother looked into her troubled, questioning eyes. "I'll tell you later," she mumbled.

"Chris?" asked June.

Mother responded with a slight shake of her head. She draped an arm around Luke and looked over at David, who was fast asleep. "Maybe we should go for an ice cream. Is anyone up for that?"

Luke bounced up and down in agreement.

"I think I'll pass," June said. "But how about after you have the ice cream I pack up Luke and take him to my house for the night? I can drop him off at school in the morning."

"That would be appreciated. Honestly, June, I don't know what I'd do without you."

"It's no problem. We love having him. Rayne is going to be here any minute to pick me up anyway."

Luke had brought a small suitcase of items like a toothbrush and a change of clothes, in case they ended up staying at the hospital with David, so he was ready for a sleepover.

Rayne arrived, and gave June a squeeze in greeting. She returned his hug, and her skirt moved enough to release the sound of tinkling bells.

"You forgot to tell me why you wear bells all the time," Luke said. "You have them on your skirts and your scarves and shoes. Why is that?"

She swayed to release the sound again. "It comes from a time when I was a little girl. My mother told me a story about spirits and the sound of bells. Evil spirits often follow children, in hopes of catching them off guard and making them do things that get them into trouble or cause them harm. She believed if I wore bells on my clothes, it alerted the good spirits to where I was and kept me safe. So I continue wearing them as a reminder of childhood, comfort, and protection."

Luke and Mother listened intently. "What a lovely story!" Mother said. "I never thought to ask why you wore them. I figured it was just because you liked them."

June smiled bashfully. When Luke and Mother left in pursuit of ice cream, Rayne looked at her with amusement.

"That is a lovely story," he said. "I never heard that one before."

"Well, I altered it a bit," she said, "but it's still the same story."

"I've known you a long time, dove, and that's not the reason your mother gives."

June shrugged nonchalantly.

"She told me the reason she put bells on your dresses was to keep track of you. You always wandered away, and she put the bells on so she could hear you from the kitchen when you were in the yard. Sort of like what people do with their cats."

June smirked. "I believe they do that to warn the birds."

He laughed. "I've grown to love that sound. Besides, it warns me that you're coming into the kitchen when I'm stealing a piece of chicken out of the fridge."

She slapped him lightheartedly on the shoulder before giving him another hug. He made her feel safe and comforted. She lowered her head onto his shoulder.

After their ice cream, Luke gathered his things together and went home with June and Rayne. Mother settled David in for the night, and sat cross-legged on the built-in bed beside the hospital bed, a feature of all the rooms. Hers connected to the wall under the window. A mattress was thrown on top of the frame, and linens and a pillow (if she was lucky) were added. Despite how uncomfortable it was for her body, it was easier on her nerves to stay in the hospital with David.

She was surrounded by books, papers, and pencils, and was underscoring passages in a textbook, when she heard the whistle coming from the hallway. It was late, past nine o'clock in the evening. Dr. Liam visited his inpatients twice a day, in addition to seeing outpatients all day in his office, but he was later than usual this evening. She heard the pull of paper towels from the dispenser after the flush of water sounded in the sink.

Dr. Liam approached them, still wiping his hands. "How's our boy?" he asked.

"He's doing better today—almost down to a half-liter of oxygen. He keeps pulling the cannulas out of his nose, and I have to place them back in when he's worked them off."

"Maybe he's trying to tell us something. Does he turn dusky around the mouth when he's off the oxygen?"

"I haven't noticed that. But I *have* noticed that his saturation levels don't change."

She glanced up at the screen that recorded vital signs. His oxygen level was at 99 percent.

"OK, I'll write an order to turn the oxygen off for a bit tomorrow and see how he does. If he can go twenty-four hours without it, you can take him home, Poole."

Dr. Liam listened to David's breathing, then strung his stethoscope back around his neck, motioning to Mother to move over so he could sit down on the cot. She scrambled to gather up all her school stuff and make room for him to sit.

He looked exhausted and distraught. In the eleven years they had known each other, a bond had been formed. Given the professional boundaries, it was not a conventional friendship, but Mother took his welfare to heart. She felt respect and love for this man, who had been the reason her son had fought his way back from deadly health-threatening situations. She waited to hear whatever he needed to say. As a physician, he possessed a strong physical core, and would find many opportunities to test it.

A few days before, Jude, his patient, had died. He offered no details about the child's condition or circumstances. "You know that Jude's parents always dressed her in butterfly clothes," he said. "She became known as Butter-jug around the office. She wore butterfly dresses, butterfly shoes, butterfly bonnets, carried butterfly blankets, butterfly toys, and had butterfly hair ties. You get the picture."

He told her that Butter-jug had been a medically fragile child from birth. In spite of all efforts made, she would not pull through this time. Her parents were prepared for her passing, and had invited friends and family to her bedside to say good-bye. They wanted to ensure she not only live a good life but would end with a good death, surrounded by those who loved her.

"Today was her funeral. It was scheduled for two o'clock this afternoon, and I was asked to give the eulogy. I arrived at the office in the morning, still trying to figure out what I could say at the funeral that might bring some peace to the family. You know my office is on the second floor, and there's no access to any windows. The only way out is via the elevator or the stairs. When I went to open the door to the office, there was a butterfly sitting on the door frame. It probably got in on someone's clothing, but I took it as a sign that Jude was letting us know she was fine. As the day progressed, with more and more parents commenting on it, I said it was a sign from heaven that Jude was happy.

"One of the moms said, 'In that case, she must be ecstatic.' I didn't know what she meant, but when I walked out into the hall, I was stunned. The upper side of the door frame was covered with so many butterflies they were starting to curve across the top. I couldn't help laughing. Now I could tell her family that without a doubt she was telling them she was fine."

Mother waited for a moment for him to continue. When he didn't, she couldn't help but ask the obvious question. "What did you do with the butterflies?"

He shrugged. "Nothing. I left them there. Something tells me Jude will guide them back to wherever they came from."

He looked David over once more, then stood with his arms crossed, leaning against the side rail. "I'll leave an order for the morning to discontinue the oxygen and see how he does."

Mother nodded her agreement. What she had just heard motivated her to ask another question. Dr. Liam's belief in the spiritual was obvious, but she wondered how strongly connected he felt to his belief. "Have you always felt that being a pediatrician was something you were meant to do?"

"You mean, do I think it was my calling?"

"Exactly."

"Yes."

"How did you know?"

"Well," he said, "you may or may not be aware that I used to be a veterinarian."

She laughed. "I kind of figured that when your waiting room occasionally has animals in it."

"I guess that *would* seem a bit unusual! Patients from my vet days often bring their pets around to my garage at home for a quick look-over. Come to think of it, I even had someone bring a horse over once."

She looked questioningly at him. "Seriously?"

"Absolutely. Several years after I graduated, I had an established practice that was going well. We had a full family, we were financially secure, and I loved what I did. Then one of my children developed serious medical problems, and was seen by multiple specialists in clinic after clinic. No one could offer definitive answers that didn't end with, 'We'll wait and see.' My wife and I were desperate, and I kept thinking there had to be a better way. In the end, I decided to pursue a career in pediatrics to help my own family, and to try and give others in similar circumstances a form of hope, and some decent answers about their children's conditions."

"Your family must be very proud of you," Mother said.

Dr. Liam shrugged. "It hasn't been without struggles."

"So you feel you're where you're supposed to be?"

"Yes. It's my gift. It's what I was meant to do."

"I wish I knew what I was supposed to do," she said. "There are so many times I feel like I'm getting nowhere—like I have a huge hole in my chest that can't be filled."

Dr. Liam stared at the floor distractedly, weighing his words, before he answered. "I know. And no matter what you try to fill it with, it won't close. Drugs, food, sex, gambling, smoking, or whatever other vices a person can think of, won't do any good. The only way to fill that vacancy in your body is to fill your soul first. You need spirituality."

Mother sat quietly, wishing she could find the same measure of comfort. "We've tried that route. We went to two different churches, and were turned away both times. Once they got a look at David, they asked us not to come back. One of my friends said it might have something to do with *Job* or *Leviticus*."

"What?"

"It had something to do with God making sinners known by punishing them with physical ailments or deformities."

"So they looked at David, and decided he was a sinner. Wow, that's twisted. But the Job story is mainly about patience, faith, and trust in God."

"In the story, I guess Job's friends believed that his plight was evidence of his own wickedness. Whatever it was, it was made clear that we didn't belong. One of the greeters, a male, wouldn't even touch my hand. He kept his hands clasped behind his back, as if he were afraid of catching something."

"Not much of a greeter, now, was he?"

He unfolded his arms and moved from David's bedside, but not before giving him a kiss on the forehead. As he turned to go, he said, "You ran into some bad luck. If you feel it may help, try it again. Our church is very accepting and community-driven. The minister, Polly, is hard-working, compassionate, smart, and very approachable. I never walk out of church without learning something. Ministry is definitely *her* gift."

"Sounds encouraging. Maybe we'll give it a try."

Mother picked up Spike, the stuffed hedgehog, from David's bed. It had taken some doing to understand what he wanted, which was to offer it to Dr. Liam. It was as if David knew some comfort was warranted.

She held the toy up to Dr. Liam. "David wants you to have this. It's very huggable."

Dr. Liam received the gift graciously. "Thanks—I'll be needing that!"

He exited the room, but not before his customary washing of hands at the sink. Mother could hear the sound of his whistle fade as he disappeared down the hall. She pulled the heavy textbook into her lap and continued to read.

Chapter 31
Panicking

~~~~~~~

Mother woke at 3 a.m. to a moaning sound coming from David. She rose from the cot, switched on the least invasive light, and looked over at him with sleepy eyes. She brushed her hand across his face, and discovered he was burning hot. Quickly switching on the invasive blaze of the overhead light, she checked the temperature of his limbs; they were hot too. His face was flushed, and his legs vibrated under the light sheet. She could hear the rise of panic in his voice as it got louder. She searched for the call bell clipped to his pillow. The pillowcase was soaked with his sweat. She pushed the bell, and tried to calm him while waiting for a nurse. Aside from the noises of the machines and David's terror, the sound that flooded her head was the beating of her own heart.

Chapter 32
Hoping

~~~~~~~~

Luke was dropped off at the hospital earlier than usual after school. A friend of Mother's had offered him a lift, so he didn't have to take the bus. She did not offer much conversation, but seemed sympathetic in her manner. "Oh, that's OK, dear," she responded, after he said "Sorry" for slamming the car door.

When he arrived at the front entrance of the hospital, he made his way through to the cafeteria, and took a quick look around in case Mother and David were there. Not seeing them, he took the elevator to the fourth floor, then wandered down the hall and past the nurses' station onto the unit. No one noticed him as he continued to David's room. He glanced a second time at the recognizable wheelchair parked to one side in a storage space, but thought nothing more about it.

He felt momentarily confused on entering the room. David's bed was missing, and the IV pole was no longer laden with pumps and equipment. He looked at Kareem's bed, taking inventory of all the items on hand, and knew at least he was in the right room. He felt doubly assured when he saw Mother's backpack lying on the cot with the zipper closed, as if she hadn't opened it all day. That was odd; normally she took her books out and studied during any spare moment.

He flopped down in the middle of the cot, and pulled his Gameboy out of his backpack. A nurse entered to remove the IV pole from the room, and appeared surprised to see him. She forced a smile when he asked if she had seen his mother. "I'll see if I can find her," she said as she exited the room.

Mother returned after a few minutes. Luke knew right away something was wrong. She removed the Gameboy from his hand so that he could listen to her. "There's a problem," she said. She waited for the words to sink in before continuing. "David is very sick. He was in surgery for nearly six hours while they tried to fix the problem. It's his colon. He has a disease in his intestine that progressed without our knowing. The disease created a hole called a leakage, and it's causing a major infection in his system."

"What does that mean? Is he OK?"

"So far. No one is panicking yet, but we're not out of the woods. They had to remove a section of his bowel and sew the major parts back together. He's in recovery right now. You're one of the faces he'll want to see when he wakes up. Do you want to walk down there and see if he's ready for them to bring him back?"

He tried hard to process all that he heard. "Where's his bed?"

"They took him to surgery on it. He'll be in a new room where he'll be away from other people. We'll have to wear a gown and mask for a while when we visit him."

"He's OK, though?"

Mother chose her words carefully. "He doesn't appear to be in any more or less danger than he usually is—at least right now."

"Why didn't you call me at school and let me know?" he asked.

"I did call the school. But I decided not to send for you unless I felt you needed to be here. David's been in surgery most of the day. Now is when both of you will need one another."

He nodded and headed for the doorway. She grabbed her backpack, and as she caught up to him, he looked up at her with frightened eyes.

"I think I should hold your hand," he said. "So you don't feel scared."

Chapter 33
Reversing

Mother heard the whistle signaling Dr. Liam's arrival. He entered the room at 9 p.m., and walked to where Mother sat huddled forward on a chair. She had lowered the side rail, and kept one hand on David's leg so that he could always feel the connection. Luke slept, curled up on the cot.

Dr. Liam reached down and gave Mother a comforting hug from the side. "Any change?" he asked.

"None, he's not responding at all."

He checked David's vital signs, pushing the IV pole out of the way. It was laden with four different pumps providing him with a host of antibiotics and other medication. A twenty-four hour nurse had been assigned to the room to monitor his condition.

Mother spoke with a sob in her throat. "It's been nearly twenty-four hours, and he's not responding. What does that mean?"

Dr. Liam shook his head. "I'm not sure. All I know is that we've taken him as far as we can. Now it's up to him and the powers that be. We just wait and hope."

The room fell void of voices. The only sound that interrupted the silence was the rhythmic beeping of the machines that connected David's small body to life.

Chapter 34
Leaving

At the doorway of David's room, Mother tossed the yellow gown into the hamper and dropped the paper mask into the garbage receptacle. She washed her hands at the metal sink, and saw the diminishing bubbles spiraling down the drain as the depletion of her energy. It had been four days since David's surgery, and he was still turned into himself. He pulled away from stimuli, such as being poked with a sharp object, but he didn't open his eyes. Dr. Liam told her that his lack of response was most likely because he was focusing his energy on healing. He also said that now was David's opportunity to decide if he wanted to remain in this life or choose to leave it. It would be easy for him to let go at this point if he wanted to. But he had had many opportunities to allow himself to die, and had never taken them. It appeared he was content with life as he knew it.

Mother stepped out into the hallway to look for Luke, who had decided to spend time in the playroom. One of the nurses approached her and asked how she was doing. "I've noticed that you've been here for nearly four days and haven't gone off of the floor for more than a few minutes," the nurse said softly. "If you don't mind me saying, maybe it's time to get away from here for a while. Take Luke for a walk, or go shopping, or maybe to a movie. It's important for you to do things for you, too. Besides, there's nothing you can do for David while he's in this state anyhow. Take a break."

"I don't think I can," Mother said. "I only feel able to take a break when June is here. I'm worried about leaving him alone."

"He's not alone," the nurse reminded her. "He has twenty-four-hour nursing care in the room, so he's under constant surveillance. Go for a walk around the grounds, or even for a pizza."

Mother considered the idea as Livia's mother passed by with a coffee, on her way to her daughter's room. Before either could speak, the paging system announced "code red, code red, 5E3, code red." *A small fire must have broken out in the cardiac station*, Mother thought, but there was nothing to worry about at this point. "If something happens, will you page me?" she asked the nurse, who immediately agreed.

Mother called out to Luke to join her. They could poke through some of the shops, visit the small library, or take a jaunt through the hospital art gallery. They made their way off the unit and onto the bridge that connected them to the main part of the hospital. She hesitated under the threatening replica of a T-Rex, and looked back toward 4C4, before forcing herself to catch up to Luke. He had run ahead to start the long walk down the spiral staircase to the ground floor. She tried to shake off her worry as she descended the stairs behind him.

Chapter 35
Regretting

They relaxed into their time together, and even went for a short walk in the garden at the front of the hospital. Both of them were hungry, and they debated whether they wanted Subway, Chinese food, burgers, or pizza from the food court. They stood in line, holding trays laden with their choices of ham-and-pineapple pizza, drinks, and a dessert for Luke.

The sound of the paging system cut through all conversation. A ping sounded, alerting everyone to hear what was coming next. "Code blue, code blue…" The cardiac team had been summoned for someone who had had a heart attack, a life-or-death situation in most cases. The announcement was followed by the location of where the heart attack was occurring—4C4.

With conscious calm, Mother placed her tray down on a table. The incident was happening on David's pediatric floor. Her eyes caught those of a server behind the counter. She felt like ice had begun to creep through her veins. The server nodded knowingly as she turned to run. She glanced back to make sure Luke was following her. Instead, looking dazed, he sat down on one of the chairs, shaking his head.

"Luke, we have to go!" she said, aware of the shrill fear in her voice.

"No," he said, shaking his head harder.

"Luke! This could be David! We have to go!"

He was crying now. "No! This is all my fault. I said I wished he wasn't born. This is my fault. I should never have said it!"

His fear had paralyzed him. She felt torn between the need to run to her older son and her responsibility to not abandon her younger child. "Luke," she said with forced calm, "we don't know if it's him, but *we have to go.*"

The ping sounded again, followed by a page for Mrs. Poole to return to station 4C4.

She sank to the floor, her mind swimming. Luke clung to her. She stood up and pulled him toward her, lifting him up into a straddle hold, so he was curved around her. He had his head buried into her shoulder, fear and tears flowing freely. She turned toward the stairs, taking one at a time. She knew this was the slowest route, but felt that it didn't matter anymore. Whatever was done was done. Luke needed her more right now.

When she got to the bridge, she put him down, then held his hand to walk to the unit. He was calmer, but still seriously distraught. As they passed the nursing unit they saw the crash cart being taken out of the room across the hall from David.

It had been someone else. Mother caught sight of Dr. Liam, standing next to Livia's sobbing mother, arm around her shoulders, saying comforting words. Mother felt as if her heart were being crushed inside her between colliding emotions of sadness and relief.

A nurse approached them and said that David had awakened, which was why Mother had been paged. She still felt the shock of the emotional wrenching, and only nodded in response.

She held Luke tightly against her, knowing the toll extracted from him. "David is awake. We can relax a little, but I think I need to be with Liv's mother for a few minutes. Can you sit with David on your own? Is it OK to ask you to do that? I'll be right in."

Luke nodded. He took a deep breath as he leaned into her. Then he broke free and headed into David's room, ignoring the yellow gown and mask as he strode up to his brother's bedside.

The room nurse watched as he pulled the side rail down and climbed in. David stirred and looked at Luke with sleepy eyes. Luke took his hand and held it tightly. Through sobs, he said, "Don't ever... do that...again."

Chapter 36
Shutting

Mother cleared their space, and put things into bags for the journey home. It had been six weeks since David had awakened from his unconscious state, and they were finally prepared to leave. The exorbitant cost of parking had her worried whether she could still make her rent without the repeated threat of eviction.

As Mother signed the discharge papers, Luke asked to take David for a stroll downstairs. He had become attentive, offering to help rather than brooding when asked. Mother didn't hurry, in order to give the boys extra time on their own, but knew she also was providing opportunity for mischief, which she saw as a part of growing. She had learned it was part of Luke's progress.

In the main foyer, Luke maneuvered David and his chair part way into the candy shop. He couldn't get the chair around the narrow aisles, so he parked David close to the doorway, where he could see him, before going in and searching for his prize. *Besides, who would steal him?* Luke rationalized. *He's too much work.*

Luke had been given some of the milk money he hadn't used due to school absences. He purchased a bag of sticky candy he had been coveting for days. The brightly coloured sugary confection had been in the shop window during one of their outings, and he was determined to buy some before they went home.

With the bag in hand, he fetched David, and pushed him into the foyer. The sun shone through the skylight canopy that loomed overhead. As they walked to the meeting point, Luke felt a strong need to use the bathroom. Quickening his pace as the urgency of his situation took hold, he hurried toward the toilets.

They reached their destination and faced the bathroom specifically designed for a disabled patron. The lock, however, claimed "occupied" in gold metallic letters. Luke hopped from foot to foot, pushing David back and forth in the chair in an effort to keep his own bladder quiet. As the door unlocked and the occupant emerged, Luke waited impatiently for the younger man to clear the doorway. He could still hear the rush of water pouring into the sink via the motion-control tap.

Luke shoved David into the large space and parked him close to the sink. He turned quickly to shut the door, only to find it was driven by hydraulics and closed at a snail's pace. Losing his patience, he leaned his body forward and shoved. Finding this effort useless, he turned and started slamming himself against it.

Once it was shut, he turned the latch and hopped to the toilet. David was in a fit of giggles, but this did not interfere with Luke's determination to relieve himself. He fought his zipper down while still gripping his bag of candy. To allow for better success, he tossed the bag toward David's lap. It landed with a plop on the edge of the white, porcelain sink just as Luke released his bladder. Relief washed over him—until his attention turned back to the bag at the edge of the sink. Its contents had shifted slightly, and it slowly slid down into the inside of the sink, toward the sensor that would release a gush of water from the tap. There was nothing he could do to stop the inevitable.

"No, no, no," he said, trying to empty his bladder more quickly by bearing down and making grunting noises. He got himself rearranged into his pants, and leapt in the direction of the sink as the open bag of candy slid further, settling into the bottom of the basin. As the bag neared the sensor, the faucet opened, filling the bag with water and drenching its contents.

Luke stood in front of the sink, looking on in despair until the gush of water abruptly stopped. He pulled out the soggy bag, now carrying a rainbow of colored candies, and slowly poured the water out. He looked at David, wrapped in happy hysterics, trying to catch his breath from laughing.

"Oh, shut it!" Luke said. He dropped the soggy bag onto David's knees before turning back to the sink to wash his hands.

They made their way to the bench near the exit doors to wait for Mother. As she approached, she could see Luke stretching something out of a bag and dropping it into his mouth. She got closer and had a better look at the disgusting mess in the bottom of the plastic bag. She stood behind David and began pushing his chair in the direction of the doorway. "You know, Luke, sometimes I think that if David could talk, you'd be in worse trouble than you usually are."

"I can't imagine that," replied Luke. He stuffed another finger full of goo into his mouth, and followed them out through the automatic doors.

Chapter 37
Trusting

Luke found water complicated, although he loved jumping and splashing around in it. He loved the feeling of resistance when he tried to run in it, and the weightless feeling he experienced when floating on top of it. But it also made him wary. Its power was evident, and it made him nervous, even in a tame environment. He enjoyed being at the swimming pool, but he didn't swim. He had never taken lessons and did not feel the worse for not doing so. "Someday," he told himself. "Someday I'll take lessons and dive off the diving board."

But it wasn't a priority. He was more enthralled with playing with David than learning a new skill. Besides, David didn't swim independently, and nobody bothered *him* about it—not that it was possible for him to do it even if he wanted to.

Luke was uncomfortable with certain kinds of risk, such as the deep end, the diving boards, and the slides, because he liked to have control of his feet on the bottom of the pool. Sometimes when Mother took David into the deeper end, where the water was above his head, he would wear his lifejacket and hang onto her shoulder, gliding along with his brother. He felt safe with the jacket on.

They went swimming every week, sometimes twice, because the physical benefits for David were immeasurable, not to mention the intense glee factor. The pool was designed to cater to the needs of handicapped children, which made the outing more than doable for their family. The Poole brothers loved their pool time.

Luke stood impatiently in the change room, making a succession of noises that echoed off of the concrete walls. He wore his favourite swim shorts and carried his lifejacket, which had his name emblazoned on the back of it in felt pen. He waited for Mother to load David into the pool chair. She hooked him up to a sling that hung from a motor suspended from the ceiling. David was dressed in swim gear, including the special lifejacket that had a section fanning out above the back of his head, to support it in the water. The lift raised him from the wide bench up into the air, like a baby being transported by a stork in a blanket. Then Mother pushed the appropriate buttons on the remote control to lower him into the chair that awaited his arrival on the tiled floor. She unhooked him from the sling, supporting his head, since the back of the chair came up only as high as his shoulder blades.

Luke belted David into the chair to prevent him from sliding out. He put his jacket and a beach bag containing towels on David's lap. As Mother attempted to push the chair, the wheels tended to wander, catching on the uneven tiles, making the effort more difficult. She pushed and Luke pulled until they stumbled their way to the pool side like a pair of tired farmhands leading a stubborn mule.

The trio made their way to the ramp that ventured downwards into the shallow end. Luke put his jacket and the towel bag against the wall, then hurried back to them. As Mother pushed the chair down the ramp, David began to squeal with delight, trying to splash as he felt the water tickle his feet.

Mother pushed the chair in farther, until David was nearly up to his waist in cool water. She undid his seatbelt, then gently tipped the chair back, the water taking most of the weight for her. The chair fell backwards and sank to the bottom of the pool, and David, lying prone, slid smoothly away from it, supported by his life jacket. The halo extension above his head kept him level, and Mother passed him over to Luke to hold him in the water. She pulled the chair up from the bottom and ran it back up the ramp to where Luke's jacket and towel bag lay against the wall.

Luke had a firm grip on the upper edge of the extension on David's jacket, and pulled him slowly in a circle through the water. David started moving his arms and legs in a slow and relaxed motion. "Feels good, eh, David?"

A large smile spread across his brother's face.

Mother took over for Luke. She pulled David toward her, standing him in the chest-high water, supporting him against her. He took weight on his legs. With the buoyancy of the water, he was able to maintain an upright posture when he leaned back against her.

Luke jumped forward in a playful manner and tagged David with his hand. "Yer it!" he shouted, and turned to run through the water in an exaggerated manner, his arms circling high. He glanced back to see if his brother was in hot pursuit.

David's legs chugged in the water, and he extended his upper body, pushing his shoulders and head back into Mother to give him momentum. She held him tight against her as he marched his way after Luke to tag him back. He was full of excitement, laughing heartily as he "ran" after his brother.

Luke slowed his pace to let David catch him, and then made a dramatic flop into the water when Mother helped David tag him with his hand. He came up, his fingers grasped firmly around his nose to prevent any chlorinated water from entering it. He hated that stinging feeling.

David tried to turn his body to run the other way. Luke dropped down again, making the sound famously associated with *Jaws*, as he advanced toward David like a shark. He dropped lower, only his narrowed eyes peeking above the water, blowing bubbles on the surface with his mouth as his body advanced in the direction of his brother.

David shrieked happily, still struggling to turn Mother around so she could maneuver him in the opposite direction. He pumped his legs and arms to try and outrun his brother, his laughter rebounding off the concrete walls. Mother ran with him, trying to reach the edge of the pool, a safety zone, before they were attacked by the great white Luke. David screamed so loud he was close to panic. The game began to take a different turn, and Mother slowed down the pace, trying to hold David calmly in the water. His mouth dropped into a pout as the game came to an end, and he started to cry.

"Don't cry, David," Luke said soothingly. He could do something silly to make David laugh, but his brother needed to relax because he had become overstimulated.

Mother lay him on top of the water and pulled him gently along by the halo of the jacket, watching as David's arms and legs relaxed. He stopped crying. His eyes closed, and his breathing slowed to an easier pace.

She looked over at the calm pool, a nearby area which had a floor operated by hydraulics. You could walk onto the platform from the pool deck and push a button. The floor would slowly drop, allowing a child to be introduced to the water slowly. The child could also be taken into this calmer pool to avoid other children splashing them, or to remove them from an active area.

Instead of going to the calm pool, Mother gave David a few minutes, gently stretching his limbs in the water. Then she stood him upright and bounced him while walking forward. As the water splashed him in the face, he closed his mouth instinctively. The bouncing was good exercise for his legs, and he enjoyed the freedom of movement in an upright position.

Eventually they both tired, so she bounced him in the direction of the hot pool, a small closed-in area with heated water in which he loved to sit. She brought him to the side where a chair-lift, called the Little Dipper, hovered over the water. With some effort, she strapped him in, then pushed a button that lifted him level with the side of the enclosure. She asked an adult sitting in the pool to hold him in the chair while she got out of the water and ran around to the steps that led into the warm, bubbling water. She relieved the kind stranger, then unstrapped David from the chair, lifting him onto her lap. They slid down slowly into the warm water so he could adjust to the temperature change. He smiled again, bubbles popping and bouncing around him, as his body seemed to melt into the warmth and comfort of the water.

Luke sat on the edge of the main pool. He clamped his nose firmly between his fingers before he dropped head-first into the water. He forced his body upward, pushing with his legs from the bottom of the shallow end, and as he broke the surface, swung his head, throwing a spray of water on a group of unsuspecting girls.

"Hey! Don't splash!" one said in a grumpy tone.

He looked at her incredulously with water dripping down his face. "You're in a swimming pool—splash happens." Then he gave her a weak smile and said, "Sorry, Tezaray."

The girl from school was a friend of Colleen's, with whom he was enamoured. Colleen had shiny blonde hair, a pinkish glow to her skin, and dark-green eyes.

"Are you here with your brother?" Tezaray asked.

"Yes," Luke replied. "He and my mom are in the hot tub."

He waved his arm in their direction, and his head followed the action. Colleen was in the hot tub too, sitting next to Mother and David, and they were chatting animatedly. Luke shook his head to remove water from his hair and crossed his arms over his chest in a protective manner, stuffing his hands into his armpits. He walked up the ramp and out of the pool, and headed in the direction of his family and classmate.

As he reached the steps that led down into the warm water, he nonchalantly called to Mother. "Mom, is it time to go yet?"

She looked up at him with a puzzled look, "No, did you want to go?"

"No. No, I was just checking," he replied as he glided down the steps.

The water was hot, but he tried to look cool, rather than shrieking and jumping back up the steps. As he adjusted to the temperature, he moved in the group's direction and sat on the ledge next to Colleen. Her hair was pulled up into a high ponytail, which hung to her shoulders. She wore a pink-and-purple one-piece bathing suit with a Hello-Kitty logo on it.

"How are you?" he asked, trying not to look too keen.

"Good!" she replied. "You have a cute brother." She poked David's belly. "You're not as serious or as grumpy as your brother can be," she said.

Luke winced. David wore his surfboarder swim shorts, and a thin undershirt to cover the G-tube that protruded from his stomach. He giggled charmingly and flashed an adoring smile at Colleen.

Luke looked past her toward his brother, with both hands in an uplifted gesture. "Really?" was the message he conveyed in body language.

David's smile brightened further, and he started making soft conversational tones to Colleen.

"He's so adorable," she said.

Luke made silent "blah, blah, blah" gestures behind her back, which made David laugh.

"Does David like the slide?" Colleen asked Mother.

"Yes. He loves it."

At the mention of the slide, David's legs started pumping. He enjoyed the excitement of it, and was able to hold his breath when he stayed dunked under water before being lifted out.

"How 'bout you? You like the slide?" Colleen asked Luke.

"Well...yeah...I guess so." He didn't want to go on it, but he didn't want to look like a coward, either.

"Let's go," Colleen said, then added, "You coming too, David?"

David was more than willing, so Mother made her way out of the hot tub with him and into the regular pool to the small slide.

Luke followed, and stood next to a group of eager children, watching, as Colleen slid down into the water.

"Come on, Skywalker, I'll catch you," a familiar voice said.

Dr. Liam stood at the bottom of the small slide with his wife and a few of his grandchildren. Luke felt uneasy. He preferred to be an observer rather than a participant. He waved away the opportunity.

Mother lifted David, and pushed him partway up the small slide. She held onto him as he slid to the bottom, then allowed him to dip under the water before pulling him up. He surfaced with his eyes closed and his face filled with excitement and joy. He loved this ride.

Colleen had had her fill of the small slide, and moved toward the diving boards, where the greater challenge lay. She motioned for Luke to follow.

Despite having no business being over there, he was intrigued. He went around the corner toward the boards, and watched as other children ran the length of the planks and jumped high, pulling their legs under them as they catapulted themselves into the crystal-clear water.

Colleen was fearless. She ran the full length of the board like a gazelle, and stretched herself upward before bouncing on the end, slicing gracefully, fingers first, into the water.

Luke gravitated toward the boards, mesmerized by the action and how easy it seemed. Children kept jumping off, returning, and jumping again. There was nothing to fear. His greatest thrill was having Colleen smile at him as she took the stairs up to the diving board.

The next time she came by she took the stairs to the high board. She made her way to the top and walked to the end before jumping off. He was so taken with what she was able to do that he didn't see Mother and David in the water on the shallow side, watching him. He went up the steps, one at a time, looking forward, feeling butterflies stirring in his belly. He would look as graceful and spectacular as she did jumping into midair and falling into the inviting water.

Reality struck as he stood at the top of the wet board, his knees shaking beneath him. The water would break his fall, but he couldn't swim. What on earth was he to do now? Maybe he would go back down.

A familiar head popped up at the top of the stairs, and Luke's body flooded with relief. "Luke, what are you doing?" Dr. Liam asked.

"I don't know. I started up the stairs and didn't want to look like an idiot, so now I'm stuck. I feel like I'm walking the plank in a pirate movie."

"I see. It never occurred to you that drowning would make you look like a bigger idiot? Your mother says you can't swim."

"Can we go back down the stairs?" Luke asked, his body trembling with fear and cold.

Dr. Liam looked back down the stairs, now filled with children waiting in line.

"I don't think that's an option any longer, Skywalker. I think you're committed to jump."

Luke closed his eyes. He felt sure he was about to cry. "Oh, my God," he said. "Why do I have this feeling that you're about to say, "Luuuke! I...am...your...doc...tor!"

Dr. Liam groaned. "It's because you watch too many movies. Look at this as a leap of faith. Trust me. We'll get through this."

Both ignored the lifeguards below, blowing whistles and motioning for them to stop.

Dr. Liam turned Luke in front of him and moved his leaden body down the plank.

"Ohmagodohmagodohmagod!" was all Luke could say. But his feet kept moving.

Dr. Liam instructed him to pinch his nose, take in a deep breath, and hold it when he hit the water. He lifted Luke, tightening his arms around his chest. "On a count of three, then. One...two...three..."

Luke heard only the beating of his own heart in his ears. There was the muffled sound of voices bouncing against the walls, and the feeling of being weightless, like a handkerchief being dropped from a great height. It seemed like an eternity before his feet hit the water and he felt himself plunging below the surface.

He came up with Dr. Liam's arms still tightly gripped around him. He madly wiped the water from his eyes with his fingers, and sucked in a deep breath of air. Dr. Liam held him up in the water so his head wouldn't go under.

"You all right?" a lifeguard asked, swimming towards them.

Luke exploded. "Holy shit! I don't believe it! That was ridiculous!"

The lifeguard got him safely to the edge of the pool, and helped him up the stairs onto the concrete. Luke was still caught up in the excitement of his act, and looked around to see Mother, David, and Colleen standing in the water not far from him. Their faces looked relieved, but then Colleen's expression changed to disbelief and Mother's to anger, and David's blossomed into a smile of adoration.

Despite the tongue-lashing he knew was coming, Luke felt like he had jumped a hurdle. He had experienced something in the worst way possible, but he also learned something: he needed to take swimming lessons.

Chapter 38
Dancing

~~~

Several days had passed since the diving-board incident. Luke had tired of hearing the jokes at school about Poole nearly drowning in the pool. In an effort to counteract his humiliation, he had signed up for swimming lessons. In time, he hoped his peers would forget it all.

His ego still smarted from his decision to climb the ladder, but, on the other hand, watching Colleen dive had thrilled him. He had avoided her since that day and was not sure how she would act toward him. He felt stupid, but there was little he could do about it now.

When the lunch bell rang, he left his desk and headed for his backpack that hung from a hook on the wall. He didn't get pizza pops often, and was ecstatic when he did. Lunch was almost always leftovers with raw fruit for dessert. Today, Mother had given him a pizza pop with a fruit roll-up for a snack. Life was good.

He didn't realize the mistake at first glance, but once he got closer, he saw that the backpack was David's. *There's no way I'm going to try and stomach a can of formula.*

He unhooked the pack and went to Miss Wong to explain the mistake. She gave him permission to take the backpack to his brother's classroom and eat lunch with David, if his teacher permitted it.

Luke made his way down the corridor to the east wing of the school. He had to ring to be let in, since the door had a locking device to prevent mobile students in the special-needs program from venturing along the hall on their own. The health-care nurse, Mrs. Bonnyville, opened the door. The children were being set up in the lunch room.

Luke grabbed David's tray, and slid it over the arm rests. "I hate to tell you, but you've got my pizza pop and I've got your liquid goo." He reached behind David, and slid his backpack off the handles at the back of the chair. He pulled up a stool and sat next to his brother as Mrs. Bonnyville started setting David up for his feed.

David's teacher, Mrs. Posey, entered the lunch area. She had lots of reddish, curly hair that bounced as she walked. She was middle-aged, sported a pair of tortoiseshell-rimmed glasses, and always wore a cheery smile. She greeted Luke warmly. "It's been a while since I've seen you, Luke. I'm glad you popped by to join us. If you need something warmed, I can put it in the microwave for you."

He thanked her, and handed over his pizza pop. While he waited, he looked around David's classroom. A few samples of the students' artwork, including some of David's, were taped to the wall. Most of the children's work was done with hand-over-hand assistance, but Luke could still see some of his brother's influence in the drawings and colour choices.

"Hey, this is nice, David," he said, walking over to one drawing with David's name neatly printed across the bottom. The lines were arched, and there appeared to be something blowing out of the top of them. It consisted mostly of blue crayon, except for a dab of pink in the centre. "Nice whale, David."

David looked surprised, but there was no verbal response.

"Oh," Luke said. "Not a whale? My mistake. Um...is it a bird?"

No response.

Luke rubbed his chin. "A bowl of blueberries?"

No response.

Luke took an exasperated sigh. "A cow...a dog...a plane...a hamburger with blue cheese and a cherry?"

David started to laugh as his brother continued to look at the picture for a clue.

Mrs. Posey returned with Luke's warmed lunch, and set it down in front of him. "What's so funny?" she asked, smiling at David.

Luke pointed at David's drawing. "What is that a picture of?"

"That's you."

Luke leaned closer to the drawing, a puzzled look on his face. "Why am I blue?"

"You're not blue. That's your blue clothes. You wear a lot of blue."

Luke looked down at his faded jeans and his blue T-shirt with Bugs Bunny on the front. "Right. What's the pink squiggle for?"

"That's your heart. He wanted to put love on you."

Luke felt a rush of warmth come over him. He looked back at the picture. He looked back at his brother. "That's awesome, dude. Looks just like me."

David grinned.

Luke settled down beside him and started eating his lunch.

"Oh," Mrs. Posey said, "you'll be interested to know that David made his choice about what option he wanted to take this term."

"What was that?"

"Well, he had a choice between shop and ballet."

Luke nodded. "Ah, David. Shop is so much fun! You get to use tools like hammers and screwdrivers and make stuff."

Luke knew that most of the building would be done by someone else, but David would be allowed to participate as much as possible. Being in a room full of wood dust and the sound of electric tools would be invigorating.

"No, no," replied Mrs. Posey, "he chose ballet."

Luke stared at her. "*Ballet*? You're kidding, right?"

"No, I'm not. I asked him four times, and he responded the same way all four times. He's the only one from class who chose it, but it's definitely ballet that he wants."

"Oh, maaan!" Luke turned to his brother. "Are you sure? That's a girly thing, David. You don't want to do that, do you?"

"Yaah," David replied.

"Seriously, dude. You're going to get laughed at."

David swung his head back toward Mrs. Posey. She snapped open a can of formula to place in the feeding bag that hung from the IV pole.

"He's made his decision, Luke. If he doesn't like it, I'm sure we can switch, but it's what he wants. Right, David?"

David smiled.

"What can he do in ballet?" Luke asked.

"Listen to the music. Interact with the other kids. His being there is not going to interfere with anyone's learning. He'll watch and participate in whatever way possible. Your mom thinks it's a great idea."

"She would. When does he start?"

"Tomorrow—right before lunch."

Luke sat thoughtfully, chewing on his food. He'd just have to find an excuse to leave the room and check it out tomorrow. He needed to know what he was up against when the teasing started. This was going to happen, and he'd have to endure it. "Ballet?" he muttered. "Oh, *c'mon!*"

The following day he confided to a few of his friends about David's new class. He watched them suppress their giggles, then present a display of manliness by pushing one another to counteract their discomfort.

They felt sorry for Luke. He was the one who was going to get teased. Why would David make such a choice? Ballet equaled sissy for a boy—it made him a target.

Fifteen minutes before the lunch break the following day, Luke asked to be excused from class. He tossed the string attached to the hall pass around his neck, and made his way to the gym stage, where he met two of his friends, Tony and Vincent, outside the door to the stairs leading to David's humiliation.

"He's in there, all right," Vincent said. "I peeked in and could see him in his chair on the stage. He's by himself."

Luke shook his head, not certain how his brother would cope with rejection. "My brother is an idiot," he said sadly as he pulled open the stage door.

They snuck their way in, and climbed the few stairs to the top of the stage floor. They hid to one side behind the heavy, red, stage curtains.

Luke saw David securely strapped into his wheelchair, positioned alone at centre stage. A pang of sorrow hit Luke's heart as he considered the abandonment of his immobile brother on the open stage.

A softly flowing melody permeated the still air. At a precise moment in the music, the ballet corps, a group of young girls from Grades 4 to

6, entered from the back of the stage. They wore leotards, tutus, and dance slippers. The dainty, fairy-like figures surrounded David as they glided his chair along with their dance movements. In the wings, the three onlookers watched in disbelief as the ballerinas spun, jumped, and posed in front of David and alongside him throughout the dance.

One dancer smiled down on him with adoration, and Luke's heart skipped a beat when he recognized Colleen. He would have done anything to get that close to her. In fact, he had already done that, having experienced near drowning in an attempt to impress her. And who was getting all her attention? David, his brother, who seamlessly sailed into any social circumstance! Why did nothing like this ever happen to him?

He stood up to see Colleen more clearly, not considering that if he could see her, she could see him. He caught her eye, and she looked back at him with confusion. The smile dropped from her face, and the motion fell from her limbs. The instructor poked her head around the corner of the curtain to see what the distraction was. Luke, followed closely by Tony and Vincent, fled unceremoniously, running down the stairs and out the door into the hall, slamming the door behind them. They bumped into one another, honking like a gaggle of ganders.

"Oh, my Gawwwd!" said Tony. "Your brother the idiot is a bloody genius! Did you see that? Did you *seee* that?"

Luke couldn't help but exhibit a smile of pride. His brother was definitely no dummy. He took huge risks, and some of them were of his own choosing.

The group made its way down the hallway toward their classrooms, pushing and shoving each other as they went, each talking without caring who else was speaking.

"I think we should hang out with David at recess."

"You mean we should hang out with the girls that will hang out with David at recess."

"Something like that, fer sure."

"Maybe we should learn to dance?"

"Oh, yeah—you'd look great in one of those stretchy things."

"It's called a leotard."

"It's called ridiculous."

"...on a guy."

The three of them entered separate classrooms, and turned in their hall passes. None of them were asked questions, because they hadn't been missing long enough. But they knew the plan for recess: take David for a walk down by the grade four lockers to see how much attention he would get from some of his fellow dancers before going outside.

Chapter 39
Wishing

Luke could not believe he was in Florida! He stood on the sidewalk in front of their villa, behind a border of bushy plants. He had smuggled a box of Cocoa Puffs and a glass of milk into the warm November sunshine. He shoved a handful of cereal into his mouth and followed it with a swig of milk to create a mixture of mush he tried to swallow quickly. Some of the milk leaked out and splattered onto his bare feet. He didn't care. He was too busy looking at his surroundings and imagining what the Disney parks would be like. He couldn't believe their luck.

The spark for this opportunity had been David's latest bout with a serious chest infection, resulting in his being put on oxygen for a short duration. Dr. Liam had asked if David had ever had a wish.

A wish? Who gets a wish? Luke thought.

David chose Disney World. It wasn't hard to determine his choice, since he almost combusted when Mickey Mouse was mentioned. Luke thought it was a good decision—it would have been his first choice, too. He didn't really understand all the preparation that went into it, but knew that everything was provided for, and it all happened quickly. They got to travel by plane, and were given access to a private room during their stopover in Toronto to allow David a place to stretch out and be changed and fed.

Once they arrived in Orlando, they drove to Give Kids the World, a resort adapted for children with disabilities. It was similar to a mini-Disney park, with rides, an ice-cream parlour, and a castle, to name just a few of the attractions. A small star with David's name on it was placed onto the ceiling of the castle, alongside thousands of other sparkling stars. Outside of the castle there was a beautifully decorated Christmas tree. Christmas all year round seemed odd to Luke, but Christmas was Christmas no matter what time of year! They were equipped with all the things David needed: medications, diapers, oxygen tanks, formula, feeding paraphernalia, and an adapted van. They also had a nurse, Judy, whom the Wish foundation had funded to accompany them and help out with David's care. They were set.

Luke could hear voices from the bungalow, and went back inside to see if everyone else was ready. He noticed Mother had a steady hand as she rinsed out her empty coffee cup and placed it into the sink, all the while humming a favourite song. Luke attributed her good mood to a better night's sleep since she shared the responsibility of David's night routine with the nurse.

Mother grabbed the heavy backpack, and headed for the door. Nurse Judy draped a plastic card on a lanyard around David's neck. His pass allowed him to be admitted to all the venues without having to wait in line. She chatted to him as she skillfully guided his chair to the van with one hand. She pulled an extra oxygen tank in a trolley behind her so that one would be on board in case they needed it during the day. Luke slipped into his sandals and hopped after them, his excitement bubbling. He found his spot in the van and buckled in. It was going to be a glorious day!

Inside the theme park, both boys felt ready to burst. Luke looked through the brochure that catered to the general public, examining options such as Splash Mountain and Big Thunder Mountain Railroad. David's brochure offered suggestions for the disabled. His ride choices were significantly slimmer, since he could not sit independently. Being on oxygen also ruled out anything with pyrotechnics. However, while Mother took Luke on some of the rides he had been desperate to experience, Nurse Judy got David a pair of Mickey Mouse ears with his name stitched on them, and a picture taken with Aladdin and Jasmine.

When Luke and Mother rejoined the pair, Luke was ecstatic. He had a jumbo ice cream in one hand and a mega drink in the other. He couldn't stop talking, and his voice was shrill when he told David all about his rides. David smiled broadly during the telling, but Luke felt a pang of guilt.

"So where do we go now?" Mother asked. "Maybe we should go to the parade?"

"Can we go here instead?" Luke asked, pointing to a ride in the brochure. The Magic Carpet ride wasn't far from where they were, and Luke thought it was something both of them would enjoy.

They headed in the direction of the ride, David pumping his legs up and down inside his straps. The golden genie lamp set high on a pole was Luke's landmark, and he headed straight for it. When they stepped into the long queue, a young lady with a Disney World badge approached them. "Does this young man wish to go on the ride? He has a pass, so we can take him right away."

This was too good to be true! Not only did they get to go on the ride, they got to go first!

The troupe followed the lady with the badge to the front of the line. "I know you won't mind," she said politely to the group at the front, "but we're going to put this boy and his family through first. We'll be with you in only a moment."

The group nodded in agreement as she scooted everyone in. She took them to the front of a car built to look like a flying carpet. Two other park employees skillfully removed the seats and set them aside. They secured David's chair onto the floor of the car with the attached ratchet straps. Nurse Judy and Luke piled into the car in front, and Mother stayed on the ground to inform the staff if the ride proved too much for David.

Luke belted himself in and kept his eyes on his brother. As the ride lifted, David's curls bounced and his head moved back. The sunshine splashed onto his face, and lit the smile stretching across it, as the carpet rose and fell. The carpets floated through the air, and Luke watched his brother shriek with delight as the ride smoothly dropped and soared, giving the feeling of flight and freedom. Luke's eyes swam as he watched David's face fill with glee and the abandonment of all restrictions as he floated through the sky, his arms flung as high as they could reach, his head pushed back in spirited laughter.

When the ride came to an end, Luke could still hear David's excited sounds, and his excitement magnified Luke's. "Want to go again, David?"

David shrieked in response.

Mother and Nurse Judy were laughing, but tearful. They seemed intrigued with Luke's suggestion, until they realized that David was slightly purple around his mouth. "He's been laughing too hard—it's impacted his oxygen saturation," Nurse Judy said. "He's in respiratory distress."

The women exchanged glances, unwittingly debating whether to send him on the ride again. Eventually common sense overrode their desire to see him so elated.

David was now overexcited, shrieking with delight as they pulled him from the ride. When he recognized that it was over, he began to cry. Luke tried to calm him by rocking the chair and making shushing sounds. Calming him would help his breathing.

Mother thanked the attendants once more as they exited the ride. They moved to a quiet spot to get reorganized, when Nurse Judy noticed that David's oxygen tank was getting low. She wasn't sure how the level had dropped so quickly, but it had. "We need to get the second tank from the van," Mother said. "Let's go to the first-aid station in case we run out before one of us returns with the tank."

When they arrived at the station, the emergency personnel on duty hooked David up to an oxygen source attached to the wall. In the meantime, an employee arrived to drive Mother to the van. His name was Auri. He was Arabic, Mother figured, in his twenties, handsome, and exceptionally kind. He drove her to the van, asking polite questions about the boys and, in particular, about David.

After returning to the first-aid station, Auri asked Mother privately if there was a character David would like to meet. She shrugged. There were so many.

Luke heard the question, and interrupted when he realized Mother was messing up a chance of a lifetime. "Mom, mom...it's Cinderella. He'd love to meet Cinderella."

"*He* would like to meet her, or *you* would like to meet her?"

Luke blushed. "No, David likes her."

"I thought he was into pirates."

"He is, but there aren't any pirate characters here. Just the ride, and he can't go on it. Trust me, it's Cinderella."

Auri smiled. "I'll see what I can do." He handed Mother a slip of paper with a phone number on it.

When they were done at the first-aid station, Luke bolted outside, looking for Auri—but he wasn't there. *Where is he...maybe a little further down the sidewalk?* Luke looked over at David, who looked calmer than he had awhile ago, and who had no idea he might be meeting a princess.

"Where's Mom?" he asked Nurse Judy.

"She'll be here in a minute."

When Mother rejoined them, they started walking in a different direction from where he thought they should go. *Shouldn't we be going to the palace? Isn't that where princesses hang out?* But he didn't say anything out loud because he didn't want to ruin the surprise for David, if there was going to be one.

Luke complained that he was hungry, and Mother got them something to eat. David happily licked candy floss off of his lip, allowing the sticky confection to melt in his mouth. Luke gnawed on a large turkey leg smothered in sauce. He thought eating would curb his disappointment, since his wish wasn't coming true. *Why did Auri promise if he wasn't going to do it?* Then he had a sobering thought. *Auri didn't promise. He said he would try.*

While eating, they stood at the back of a lot, next to a ten-foot fence with a set of heavy wooden gates. A man wearing a white wig tied at the nape of his neck with a ribbon, and dressed in a light-blue period costume, approached them. He asked Mother if she and her "subjects" would follow him.

The large gates were pulled open, and they all went through into a beautiful garden. Auri stood inside. He greeted them, then gestured for them to follow a paved path that wound through the tall trees. The boys looked around, trying to figure out where they were: and then they saw her walking up the path towards them. Her blond hair was piled on top of her head, and she had a wide blue ribbon tied around it. She wore a full-skirted blue dress that sparkled in the light and swept alongside as she walked, making her appear like she was floating. Her smile melted the boys' hearts as they waited for her to reach them. Neither was prepared for the importance of the moment. They forgot that David's face had spots of pink candy floss stuck to it, and that Luke's face was smeared with sauce. They still looked bright and eager, and their eyes gleamed with anticipation as she held out her arms, inviting an embrace. Frozen with elated anticipation, neither of them could breathe.

Chapter 40
Winning

Winter arrived. Since it dominated the seasons, winter sports tended to dominate as well. Snowmobiling, ice fishing, skiing, snowboarding, hockey, tobogganing, sledding, and ice skating were things Luke enjoyed whenever he could. The expense of many winter sports forced Mother to shy away from most of them, with the exception of skating. She owned a pair of old, white figure skates, scarred with ankle wrinkles, and scuffed at the front from hitting too many rink boards. Although she liked skating, she wasn't accomplished, but she wanted the boys involved in some outdoor sport that offered good exercise and fresh air. She also liked the anonymity of skating. For the most part, no one paid attention to them. Besides, there was a rink in the community, and Luke often went after school or in the evenings with his friends if he was waiting for her. He might not be much of a swimmer, but he had become a strong skater.

One evening, when the snow was heavy but the temperature relatively mild, Mother drove the boys to an ice rink in the river valley. In the summer, it was a large pond with an island of shrubs and plants in the middle, which made for a circular skating track around it in the winter.

In the parking lot, Mother hoisted David out of his chair, and carried him to the edge of the snowy path that led to the rink. Luke stood on the path with a toboggan, and waited for her to lay David on it and tie him in. He pulled the sled easily on the packed-down trail to the edge of the rink. Mother caught up, carrying a blanket, a pillow, two thick cardboard boxes, and two pairs of ice skates. Dropping her cargo, she opened one of the boxes, taking out a carrier that contained a thermos of hot chocolate, a few sandwiches, a can of formula, and a large 60-cc syringe to plunge David's food directly into his G-tube. They planned an *al fresco* meal after their skate.

Mother placed the items on the bench, and watched Luke take off with expertise. *He's good on skates*, she thought. He had good control moving forward and backward, and could even do a crossover turn with agility and ease. He had grown considerably this year, and was tall for an eleven-year-old. He took off like a rocket, turned, and sped toward them, arms swinging and legs pumping hard.

David squealed; he knew what was coming.

"Luke, don't!" Mother said, knowing it was a hopeless request.

Luke stopped abruptly in front of them and plowed his blades into the ice, spraying ice and snow onto David's prostrate body on the sled. David exploded into laughter as the droplets landed on his face and eyelashes. Mother tried to wipe them off with her scarf.

"Oh, Luke, go for a skate and come back in a minute," she said. "Don't bother me right now—but be careful and don't go too far," she added as he sped away.

The rink lights sparkled to life as Luke made his way around the ice in the twilight. There was music for the skaters, but he tended to ignore it. He cautiously dodged in and around them.

As he rounded the second bend, a group of boys from school came into sight. There were Marcus, Vincent, Evan, and Hektor, the bully he had punched last year for making fun of David. There had been encounters since them, especially about David taking ballet. He wasn't sure how Hektor had found out about it, but he had his suspicions: he was never sure on which side Vincent stood.

Although bothered by it, he ignored the other boys. He wouldn't give them the impression they had ruined his evening, but he'd have to keep one eye on them at all times—even though he was willing to bet he could outskate them.

Returning to Mother and David, he watched her finish, tying her laces around the top of her skates. She pulled the boxes onto the ice, placing one inside the other for strength. The inside box was a lid from a container of oranges she had taken from one of the local supermarkets: it read "California Oranges" in orange print, and pictured a few of the fruits on the side. But the outer box boldly advertised Tampax as its previous contents.

Luke jumped back when he saw the box. "Mom, no, you can't put him in that!"

"What do you mean? It's just a box."

"What's wrong with the oranges box? Put him in the oranges box instead." His mind flitted toward Hektor and his gang on the ice.

"I don't see what the fuss is. You can't stack them the other way. The oranges box is too small for the other to fit into."

"Then just use the oranges box, Mom." He threw one of the blankets over the Tampax box to remove it from view.

"It won't be strong enough, and it will fall apart too soon," she said, but against her better judgment, she deferred to Luke's decision.

Luke shrugged his shoulders, and continued to prepare David to go into the heavy orange box. There was no *way* he was going to put his brother in a Tampax box.

He pulled the cardboard box onto the ice. Mother picked up David from the toboggan and placed him in a crisscross sitting position inside the box. Then she took the blanket and pillow, and stuffed them around David to hold him upright and cushion the back of his head. He was still able to see over the edge of the box and view where he was going.

Mother leaned forward, and began pushing the box along the ice. David turned his head to view the other skaters going past, while light flakes of snow fell onto his red, maple-leaf toque and red-and-white mittens. Luke followed, doing silly, amusing things, or skating in circles around them as they moved along. The box slid easily on the clean ice, but wetness was its enemy, so its lifespan would be short. Still, this makeshift sled allowed David to sit upright and enjoy a short period of fun before his cardboard chariot disintegrated into a sloppy mess.

People passed them on the ice, and a few skaters looked back with friendly smiles and acknowledging nods. As they came around a corner, Luke caught sight of the boys from school, standing in a line by the island at the centre of the frozen pond.

"Once around, and then back here for the winner!" Evan said, pointing to the skating shack across from them. Clearly they were about to run a race.

Then they saw Luke, skating alongside David and his cardboard box. "Hey, Poole!" Hektor said, pointing at the picture of the oranges on the outside of David's ride. "What's in the box? *A fruit?* You got a retard *fruit* in that box, Poole?"

Luke had learned that the two most upsetting taunts were to call someone "gay" or "stupid." He didn't understand how being homosexual or being delayed made you lower than anyone else, but going as low as possible was where Hektor always went.

"That boy's being horrible!" Mother said. "I'm going to say something."

"No, just ignore them," Luke said, but inside he was steaming.

"Hey, Loser Luke, want to race and get yourself beat? You're such a weirdo." Hektor continued shouting, despite frowns from other skaters passing by.

Vincent removed himself from the group and skated to the boards, ostensibly to fix his skate. Meanwhile, without waiting to see if Luke was interested in the invitation, Evan counted down. Evan, Hektor, and Marcus took off together in a mad rush down the ice, with Hektor in the lead.

Luke's mind filled with the image of himself standing on the edge of a diving board, filled with excitement and dread. *The only thing worse than losing is not trying.* He skated up behind David's box and pushed him forward and away from Mother's hands, much to her surprise. "Come on, Juicy Fruit, let's race," he said to David. "Besides, you owe me one. You could be sitting in the embarrassing box right now."

Luke leaned into the cardboard, pushing with all his might, his legs pumping violently, moving at an ever-increasing speed. They rounded the bend, and he could see the boys thrashing ahead of them. He steered David clear of other skaters, and pressed on. The cargo in the box in front of him screamed as Luke heightened their speed, passing Evan after the first turn. They sped past benches, other skaters, and people staring at them from the sidelines. Luke pressed on, gaining on Marcus as they entered the next bend in the rink. The box was starting to sag, and wetness was penetrating the cardboard. How much longer could it last?

His mind raced along with them, summoning images and remembered dialogue. *I'm sorry, Cap'n, but I can't hold'er much longer! I think she's gonna blow!* Scotty from *Star Trek* had always been one of his favourites.

He went into the bend, and as his body took the curve, he released one arm from the box, using it to propel himself faster. It shot out like a windmill and his legs scissor-crossed to give him greater momentum around the corner. His head was down, his body bent forward, and he pressed on, with David still screeching from inside the box in a mixture of excitement and fear.

Hektor was ahead, skating hard and almost at the skating shack, the finish line. Luke could feel the cardboard give again, and the bottom of the box beginning to spread. He gave one final burst of speed as Ethan and Marcus rounded the corner to witness his expected defeat. He was shoulder to shoulder with Hektor, meters away from the shack. Like a couple of race horses, they plowed on. With moments to spare, Luke passed Hektor, then shot past the shack like lightning. His arms went up in the air in victory for a fraction of a second—and then the box collapsed. The bottom split, and its contents spilled out, sending David, a blanket, and a pillow spinning down the ice. Luke tripped and headed after him, both boys crashing into a snow drift at the end of the rink. The impact sent puffs of snow into the air, which showered back down on them as if from a whale's spout.

Luke could hear Hektor yelling. "You suck, Poole!"

"You're a loser, Hektor!" he shouted back, still lying prostrate on the ice.

"Yah?" responded Hektor. "Well, you can kiss my—," and he slapped his bottom as he skated away, with Marcus and Ethan guffawing behind him.

Vincent joined them a moment later. People frowned at them, but no one said anything as they exited with a banner of verbal obscenities flapping around them.

Luke got up to check David, whose arms and legs thrashed in the snow, an indication nothing was broken. "Oh, you want to go again?" David squealed with delight. Luke laughed. "Sorry, bro, I'm afraid your carriage has turned back into a pumpkin." He looked back at the soggy cardboard box, and the blanket and pillow lying on the ice.

Mother skated toward them. Her arms were stiff, and she was moving a lot faster than she normally did, walking more than skating, one foot placed in front of the other in a quick, jerky fashion. Her body was hard, but her face softened as she got a good look at them. "Are you both still alive?" she called as she approached.

Luke repeated her words in his head. He grabbed one of David's legs and dragged him out onto the ice, looking for the sled to take him back to the car. "*Both* safe and sound, Mom!"

His brother gave him a beaming smile that melted his heart. The snow fell like white stars landing softly all around them. They waited for the low light of approaching dusk to embrace them, and for their mother's concern and pride to finally reach them.

Chapter 41
Choosing

Luke plunked himself down on the frost-covered bench and began pulling off his skates, while watching Mother. She plumped up a pillow behind David so that he was not lying flat on the sled, victim to an onslaught of wet snowflakes landing on his face. She removed the sandwiches and hot cocoa from their picnic lunch.

With his boots back on his feet, Luke tied his skates together, and straddled them over the back of the bench. He looked at Mother's skates beside them and relished in the glory of his win. He bit off a piece of his sandwich, and thought about his brother as he chewed. "Mom, do you think David feels bad that he can't skate?"

Her straightforward answer made sense and made him feel better. "I don't think you can miss doing something you've never done. Besides, what makes David so unique is that he finds happiness in any opportunity he's given and that joy spills over onto others. And don't forget that he does skate—he just does it in a creatively different way."

Luke took a swig of the hot chocolate, then placed the container under his brother's nose to let him inhale the glorious scent. He pulled up a drop of the liquid from the edge of the thermos mouth and placed it on David's lips. "So delish, David!"

The trio sat in silence, enjoying the time together. Luke was the first to break the silence. "Mom," he asked hesitantly, "do you love us the same?"

It took her a minute to catch the impact of the question and regain her composure. "The simple answer is that I love you differently," she said. "You are very different people. The things I love about you are not the same as the things I love about David."

"But let's say we were in a car accident and you could only save one of us. Who would you save?"

"*Sophie's Choice*," she said softly.

"What does that mean?"

"It's a very heart-wrenching story about a woman in a war camp who is told that she can only save one of her children. She has to choose between them."

"How would you choose?"

"You're young and probably won't understand this, but the story should have been called *Sophie's Dilemma*. A choice is between two things that are nice, like apple pie or vanilla ice cream. A dilemma is more often between two things that are not nice, like getting divorced or living with someone who doesn't respect you."

She stopped as she saw confusion fill his face, and thought for a minute. "OK, how about this—it's like making a decision between being eaten by a tiger or jumping into a roaring fire. "

"You mean you'd save David."

"No. I'd save whomever needed me the most."

"Which is David."

"Not necessarily. The connection between me and you is different than the one I have with David. I have to give you independence. I have to allow you to make mistakes, try things for yourself, and trust that you'll pull through. There's no question that David can't be independent and that he relies on me for almost every breath he takes. It's a powerfully tight connection, with little wiggle room."

"So you'd save David."

She felt no anger at the question her son had thrown at her. It was more an opportunity to explore her feelings, and for both her sons to recognize the love extended to them. "Luke, I have to hope you have what you need to get yourself out of bad situations. I'd be the voice in the dark to guide you, but I hope that, physically, you'd look after yourself. The bottom line is that I'd never abandon you if you weren't safe, but I would hope you'd use your brain and body to help yourself."

"So you don't love one of us more?"

"Absolutely not. It's more about which one of you would need me more at the time. My love for you both is not a contest, it's a given. You confuse my physical attention to David as love, when his life depends on that attention for his survival. If I had to make a decision between you both, I'd help the one who was in the most danger."

Luke breathed in, and felt sure his lungs could expand further than normal. Much of his self-doubt floated out of him when he exhaled, and he felt relieved.

Chapter 42
Frightening

Leaves were falling from the trees, and the earth was changing; the air was crisper, and the sky grew dark a little earlier every day. A year had passed since Livia's death, September 2 at 5:22 p.m.

Within a week of that date, there had been a church funeral, attended by nearly three hundred guests. After the service, everyone gathered outside for the scattering of some of her ashes in the church garden. A congregation member noticed a spotted ladybug on her shirt, and pointed excitedly to it and its seven spots. Other ladybug sightings occurred on a shoe, a coat, in someone's hair, and on the windshield of a car. Livia's totem, or animal spirit, thereafter became the ladybug, just as Jude's had been the butterfly. Ladybugs would serve as a reminder for Livia's mother, especially those with seven spots.

Now, on the anniversary of Livia's death, Mother scuffed her way through the fallen leaves to load the van with essentials for the day they would be spending at Rhonda's home. They had been invited to gather in Livia's memory, and to share their support at this difficult time.

"Luke, take these boxes and put them in the back of Smog, please," Mother said. "You'll have to move all the swim gear out to get them in."

Luke filled his arms, grabbing a lifejacket, a flipper, a mask, and three flotation noodles, and set them in the basement. He was tired already. After several trips, he had successfully placed the boxes filled with supplies for David, food for the party, and a board game into the back of the van. Mother said their dog could go along this time, so he went back inside to get Goliath.

At Rhonda's house, Luke was surprised to see a number of other children around his age all gathered in the basement rumpus room. They brought David down on Livia's lift that had been added when she became too heavy to be lifted downstairs. With David included, the group of five played games, ate snacks, told jokes, and horsed around, leaving the adults to chat in the kitchen and living room. Following dinner and the fine speeches in Livia's honour, the children moved back into the rumpus room, and laid themselves out on the sofas.

"I am *soooo* stuffed," said Brian, an eleven-year-old who was tall for his age. He wore glasses, perched on his aquiline nose. His brown hair was too long and hung over his ears, and he wore a dark-red argyle sweater that clashed with a pair of chocolate-brown dress pants and blue striped socks.

"Me too!" said Mark, as he rubbed his distended stomach. He had milk-white skin, fine features, and straight, white-blonde hair that hung in front of his face, shielding his eyes. He frequently flipped his head to one side to throw aside his bangs. When his eyes were uncovered, bright-blue gems shone below pale-blonde lashes. He was thin, small, and dressed in faded jeans, a western shirt, and an oversized jean jacket.

Samantha kept her eyes on her feet. She scraped a few strands of her auburn hair behind her ears, then folded her arms tightly across her chest. Her hair had been crimped, and her long tresses, which fell almost to her waist, followed a wavy pattern. She wore a crisp, mint-green blouse with a purple, floral skirt. Her ears were adorned with small pearls, and a sparkling gem dangled from a chain around her neck. There was the faint appearance of gloss on her lips, which flattered the pinkness of her fair skin.

David sat in his chair, with his head pressed to one side of the headrest. His eyes were closed; he appeared to be asleep. Goliath sat next to him, his blond head in his master's lap. David's hand rested gently on the giant retriever's head.

Luke, who would soon celebrate his twelfth birthday, lay flat on his back on the sofa. His feet were pushed up against Mark, and he groaned dramatically. "I think I should have passed on that last helping of potatoes and gravy. But it was so good!"

Everyone else, with the exception of David, giggled.

"So what do you want to do now?" Luke asked, forcing himself upright.

"We could watch TV or play some video games!" Brian said.

No, thought Luke. He wanted something with a little more adventure in it. "Is there a park or something close by we could visit?" he asked.

"Not really. And it's getting kind of dark. I doubt my mom would allow me out now anyhow."

Luke sank back into a state of glumness, not sure what he wanted to do.

"You're right," Mark said. "It *is* a bit dark out now, and the only place close by would be the cemetery."

Luke's back straightened, and his head swiveled. "Cemetery? Who in here doesn't want to go to a cemetery?"

Mark began to raise his hand, but changed his mind when no one else raised theirs.

"Oh, c'mon! We *have* to do this!"

No one else seemed to harbour the same enthusiasm.

"We'd have to clear it with our parents, and I know mine would say no," Brian said.

Luke inclined his head toward where the adults were gathered. "Be a hero. Just ask."

Brian made no effort to move, so Luke jumped off the couch and headed upstairs. No one followed him.

He found Mother sitting on one side of the cleared dining-room table. "Mom, we were thinking of going for a walk. That OK with you?"

"Where were you going to walk to?" she asked.

"Oh...just around. Nowhere very far. We thought we'd work off some of the awesome dinner." He patted his stomach.

"Well, I guess it's OK if you take an adult with you."

Luke felt his body deflate as he exhaled.

"So we can't go by ourselves?" he asked, knowing that an adult wouldn't take them to the cemetery in the approaching darkness.

"No. You need someone older to go with you."

He rolled his eyes and went back to the rumpus room, flopping himself onto the couch. "We can't go unless we have somebody older with us."

The group sat silently considering their situation.

"How old is Goliath?" Brian asked sarcastically, causing Samantha to giggle.

Luke's forehead furrowed in concentration as he turned his gaze toward his brother and their dog. "Goliath is fifty in dog years," he said. "But...David...hmmm."

He looked at the others. "How old is everyone?" He pointed at each of them in turn.

"Eleven," said Brian.

"Eleven," Samantha replied.

"Nine," said Mark.

"Soon to be twelve!" Luke pointed to himself. "Soon to be thirteen," he said, pointing to David.

No one responded.

"Well!" Luke said, jumping onto his knees on the sofa. "David is almost thirteen, so that makes it all OK!"

"Luke, you can't be serious. David can't be responsible for us. He's disabled," Brian whispered.

"Minor detail—who still wants to go?" Luke threw his arm triumphantly into the air.

Mark's hand hesitantly followed, and eventually so did Samantha's. Luke ran over to David and raised his hand for him. "Come on, Brian! It'll be fun."

"If your Mom says we can go, then fine," Brian said reluctantly. "But tell her who our babysitter is."

Luke dashed upstairs to find Mother. "What age do you have to be to babysit?" he asked.

She had to think for a minute. "I think it's thirteen," she said uncertainly.

"I think so," said Rhonda. "Thirteen or fourteen."

"One of the kids is going to be thirteen in a few weeks. Can we all go out for a walk together?"

Mother assumed he meant Brian. He was certainly the biggest, and seemed to be a sensible sort. "It's OK with me, but you have to check with the other parents. And don't be gone long; just around the block a couple of times and back."

Luke agreed, and after a quick check with the other parents, who were more involved with their own conversations, he ran back to the rumpus room with the news.

They pushed David outside in his chair, then zipped up their jackets and exited the yard. The air was cool, and the sky had a purple tint as darkness approached. Goliath jogged alongside David's chair as Luke maneuvered his brother down the sidewalk. Everyone helped in getting the chair up and down the curbs and over sidewalk cracks that made the wheels stick.

Their conversations varied from how big dinosaurs really were to how cool Michael Jackson was. Mark even stopped to give an impressive demonstration of his moonwalk.

They reached the cemetery gates after walking four blocks. The gates were closed and a loose chain hung between them. It looked like the set of a horror film.

"It's locked. Guess we have to go back," said Brian.

"No, it's not," Luke replied. He reached for the chain and pulled it through, clanking it noisily along the metal gate. The gate creaked in response as he pushed it open. A gust of wind blew dried, rustling leaves across their path. Luke pushed David through the entrance, along a dirt path with tire tracks worn into it, and the rest of the group followed them into the growing darkness.

Trees bordered both sides of the path for several feet. Beyond them, they could see the shadowy shapes of the crosses and stones that marked the gravesites of the dearly departed. In the daylight, the cemetery was a beautiful, peaceful place, filled with plants, flowers, and manicured grass. At night, though, it was filled with mystery and fear, at least in the growing imaginations of children curious about scary stories.

A path snaked off in another direction, and they followed it, walking slowly and carefully, checking over their shoulders for whatever might be sneaking up from behind.

"Have any of you ever seen a ghost?" asked Luke.

Brian shook his head.

"I did once," replied Samantha. "You know that old house by the railway tracks on Wisteria Way?"

"The one where that old guy hung himself because he lost all his money and his family left him?"

"Yes, that one."

Everyone nodded. It was an old, two-story home with a front porch and a crumbling, concrete sidewalk. It had been a beautiful home in its day. Dark-green ivy scaled up one side of the wall, next to the big picture window. The spade-shaped leaves wound themselves around the drainpipe that climbed up to the eves, their stiff stems making a scratching sound against the metal. A tangle of lilac bushes grew on either side of the front steps, almost obscuring them from view. The roof was in ill repair, and many of the shingles and boards were missing.

"Chloe, Mark's sister, and I went in there once," Samantha said. "You're not supposed to—there are signs that say 'Danger, Keep Out!'—but we got over the fence and went in anyway. We tried the doors, but they were locked, so we got up on the timber box under the kitchen window at the back and climbed through. The inside of the house was a mess, just the way he left it twenty years ago, some people say. There was old furniture, newspapers, clothes, and pieces of broken glass all over the place. We heard something upstairs. Chloe said it was probably pigeons and that there was nothing to be scared of. I didn't want to go, but she said we were there so we should go upstairs and check it out. You know—where he did it."

"Where he did what?" asked Luke.

Samantha made a gesture of pulling on a rope at her neck, and hung her tongue out to one side.

"Oh! Where did he do that?" asked Luke.

"In the attic."

"You and Chloe went into the attic?" Mark asked. His respect for his older sister was rising.

"Sort of. There was this ladder built on the wall in the hallway upstairs. It went up to a board that slid across in the ceiling. If you climbed the ladder you could move the board over and go into the attic."

"Did you go?" Luke asked, feeling the hair on the back of his neck start to bristle.

"We tried to. Both of us went up together and pushed the board out of the way. I could see past Chloe, and when we opened it, bats started to fly around. There were feathers everywhere."

"You mean pigeons," Mark said. "Bats don't have feathers."

Samantha ignored his comment. "You could see through the roof in spots, which is how the bats got in, I guess. In the dim light, I thought I could see a rope hanging from the rafters, and all of a sudden we were hit with a burst of wind and couldn't see 'cause of all the dust. Then the rope started to move." She used her hand to demonstrate a slow, rhythmic motion.

The boys stopped in their tracks, and Goliath sat beside David, patiently waiting for them to start again.

"Why did the rope move?" Brian asked.

"It was the ghost," Samantha whispered, "swinging from the rope. Then that chilly wind blew past us again, and the door at the end of the hallway slammed shut." She clapped her hands together.

The boys jumped.

"The door at the other end of the hall slammed shut too." She slapped her hands again, and the boys jumped once more.

"Then what happened?" Brian asked.

"We practically fell down the ladder and ran down the stairs. We climbed back out of the window. We could hear the scratching sound by the front door as we raced out of the yard. It was like the house was telling us not to come back. We ran all the way home."

"Oh, my God," said Luke. "Did you see anything on the end of the rope?"

"You mean like a ghost-on-a-rope?" Mark said with a snicker.

"Very funny, ha ha."

"No. We just saw the rope moving."

"It could have been the wind through the roof," Brian said.

"What about the voice telling them not to come back?" asked Luke.

"It wasn't a voice," Samantha said impatiently. "It was more of a spooky scratching sound."

Regardless of the explanations, all members of the party were suddenly more sensitive to the sights and sounds in the graveyard. Without further conversation, they carried on their way, the moon shining above them in the still twilight.

As they wound their way to the end of the cemetery, Samantha broke the quiet. "Have *you* ever seen a ghost?" she asked Luke.

"No, I haven't, but David has."

"How do you know he has?"

"Well, he hasn't seen a ghost exactly, but Mother says he sees spirits."

"What does that mean?" asked Mark.

"Sometimes, he'll start talking to the air, like he's talking to someone, only he uses sounds, not words. My Aunt June says he communicates with the spirits. He does it at the hospital, in his room, or even at the grocery store. He just all of a sudden starts making talking sounds and stares at a certain spot in the air."

"So how do you know he's talking to spirits?" asked Samantha.

"Mother says that disabled kids, babies and animals, are more sensitive to things like that. They pick up on energy easier than we do. If our cats or our dog are in the room with him, they stare at the same spot he does. It's spooky."

"Wow," said Mark.

"So...why don't we try it?" Samantha asked. "You know, let him contact the spirits in the cemetery."

She didn't think anyone would take her up on it, but Luke studied David. "OK, why not?" he said. "Let's try it. What do you think, David?"

David cocked an eyebrow. He pulled his head to one side and tried to get a grip on Goliath's fur.

Luke turned David's chair around and took him off the path. He bumped him across the uneven ground and a few gravesites, stopping in front of a large, weathered tombstone, flanked on either side by overgrown peony bushes. The tall grey stone had a Celtic cross carved into the top. The owner's name was Joseph McGavins, and he had died in 1964. Luke made a quick apology for walking on the grass of the grave, then turned David around again to face him.

"OK, we want you to talk to his spirit. His name is Joe. Just call this guy and have a talk with him. We're going to wait over there and watch. If there's any trouble, Goliath is right here. He'll protect you."

At that, Luke put on the chair brakes, turned abruptly, and jogged back to the others waiting on the path.

"Let's hide behind here!" Mark said, and the group ducked down behind a large bush close to the road way.

David sat in his chair, looking upward at the night sky. The variations in shade of the inky blackness and smoke-coloured clouds intensified the beauty of the luminous moon that peeked out from the dark canvas of the heavens. He breathed a big sigh, and waited for something to happen. He wondered when they were going home. It was late and it was dark, and he was ready for bed.

He shifted his head, looking for Luke, but no one was around. There was only him and Goliath. He breathed another sigh and, out of boredom, started to hum. He wasn't sure what the song was, but he started it at a low pitch, enjoying the vibrations in his throat and the differences in sound.

The group behind the bush hushed one another and kept still. They didn't know what was happening, but felt certain David was calling a spirit from another world.

He became more involved in his singing, and experimented with different sounds and levels of pitch. Sometimes the sound imitated the call of a screech owl. As he became more involved with his singing noises, he started to move his wrists and ankles, straining them against the straps. He felt lost in his own world of noise and movements, unaware of the stifled cries and building tension behind the bushes only a few feet away. He heard a rustling sound just before his big finish and stopped abruptly, holding his breath and looking in the direction of a shrub.

The group huddled with their hands over their mouths, watching Goliath stand alert, his eyes on the same spot. He emitted a low growl. The tension was broken when he barked loudly and darted in the direction of the peony plant, pouncing onto it with all four feet. David screamed, and the group jumped out of the bush, shouting and running in all directions, shattering the stillness of the graveyard.

A small furry creature with long ears darted in front of them, with Goliath in hot pursuit, both animals bounding across the grounds.

"Shit, shit, shit!" Brian said, as he held his chest and flopped down on the grass near David.

Samantha gasped through fingers folded in front of her face. "What was that?"

"Whatever it was, Goliath is after it," Luke said, making his way to David, now in full crying mode after being left alone and startled by all the barking and shouting. Luke rocked the chair in an effort to soothe him, and gave him a hug while softly hushing him.

Mark stood close by, hunched over, his hands pushing against his knees to hold himself upright. "Holy crap," he said, "what the hell was that?"

Brian lay on the ground with one arm flung over his eyes, still trying to slow his breathing. "It was a rabbit, you guys. Not a spirit, not a ghost, not a zombie...a rabbit. A fluffy bunny, for God's sake!"

Luke shouted for Goliath as the group made efforts to collect itself. Having calmed David, he started pushing him along the path again. Goliath, back with the posse, trotted alongside, supporting David's hand with his head.

On the way out, Luke studied the messages on the headstones. They revealed a shared pattern of sentiment: 'Sadly Missed,' 'Forever Remembered,' 'Eternally Loved.' This was not a place of fear and fright; it was a place filled with love and loss.

The group made its way back to Rhonda's house, pushing one another and laughing about how scared they had made themselves. They had been gone for less than an hour. They got David back down into the rumpus room and made themselves comfortable. Rhonda brought down a tray of strawberry-shortcake desserts, and passed them around. They all tucked in; the only sounds were the scrapping of metal spoons on stoneware or the occasional grunt of appreciation.

David sat in his chair near a lamp that shone on his face. He looked like a Rembrandt painting under the soft golden light. At his feet, Goliath rested his great head on his paws.

David moved his head, and smiled as the group licked remnants of berry juice and whipped cream from their fingers. His gaze shifted sideways, and he took in a breath of air. "Hhhhi." His breathless manner caused Goliath to raise his head and look in the same direction.

Luke watched his brother in the haze of soft light. David continued with his sounds, as if he were having a conversation, although it was gibberish. The other children's attention was committed to the TV, but Luke's eyes remained fixed on David and Goliath. David turned his head to the other side of the chair, his smile still radiating, but his eyes were now trained on a different spot. Goliath sat up and turned his head in unison with David, who began to laugh as he breathed in deeply. Luke walked across the room and stood in front of David, waiting for his brother to acknowledge him. "Is that Livia?" he asked. "Is she here?"

"Yah," David replied. His eyes glanced in the other direction before returning them to Luke.

Luke looked at Goliath. Something moved on his collar. He leaned down for a closer look, and saw a ladybug making its way past the leash hook. He knelt in front of David, feeling an overwhelming love, and ran his fingers through Goliath's fur, while looking into the animal's brown eyes. He extended one finger and lifted the small insect from the collar, then got to his feet and faced Brian, Samantha, and Mark.

"Hey, you guys," he said. "It's a ladybug."

Samantha went over for a closer look.

"How many spots?" asked Mark.

"Seven."

"Cool! That means it's seven years old."

It actually doesn't, Luke thought. But it had the same number of spots as the ladybug that was first seen at Livia's funeral.

He sat on the floor next to his brother and leaned his head against Goliath, watching the ladybug on his finger. Without warning, its wings appeared. David made a sound, and the tiny bug took flight, disappearing into the room.

Mother's voice called to them from down the hall. It was time to go.

"Too bad we didn't get to see a real spirit," Brian said.

"You're right," Luke replied. His eyes met David's, and he saw something he'd never seen before: a quietness that resonated in his brother's gaze—a knowing.

The other kids followed David and Luke upstairs to say goodbye.

"Brian, I understand you have a big birthday coming up," Mother said.

Brian looked at her with a frown, and shook his head.

"Aren't you going to be thirteen soon?"

Brian shook his head again.

Luke quickly pushed David over the threshold of the back door, and strode briskly down the walkway toward the van.

"Luke? Luke? Who was the babysitter?"

Luke rounded the corner, and headed to the van at a run with David in front of him. The chair bounced on the uneven sidewalk, and both boys got caught up in a fit of giggles as the sound of Mother's questions faded into the background and drifted away with the breeze.

Chapter 43
Remembering (2002)

A lot of talking roused Luke from his fog. He was slouching in a chair on the aisle in Dr. Liam's front garden. He pulled himself up to sit properly, and saw that the yard was full of people. He rubbed his eyes, and glanced at the empty chair next to him. A man sitting nearby told him she had gone to make another phone call and would be back shortly. The man expressed his condolences. "I'm so sorry about what happened."

Luke nodded and turned away, emotion stinging the back of his throat. He looked up at the screen showing the picture of a handsome young boy, his name typed across the bottom. Dr. Liam would be calling the family to say a few words about their son, who had passed away several months ago. It felt warm under the tent canopy, and he shielded his eyes. Although the glorious sun shone brightly, his thoughts returned to rain, windshield wipers, and a sound like a gunshot.

Chapter 44
Raining

Luke put two plastic bags of groceries into the back of the van, then ran around to the passenger door and jumped inside. David was already strapped in, ready to go, but Mother had gone back inside the shop for a forgotten item. The sky had begun to darken after a hot day, and he expected it would probably rain.

Sure enough, a few drops hit the windshield as Mother emerged. She wore his Hulk T-shirt, and had her slicker still tied around her waist. She climbed inside, and motioned for him to take his spot behind her on the bench. He was safer there, and could also keep a better eye on David. She pulled Smog out of the parking lot and onto the street just as the rain suddenly started to fall like it was being dropped from buckets. She switched the windshield wipers on high and headed in the direction of the bridge they would cross on their way home. "I'm sorry," she said, "but it looks like we won't be making the picnic in the River valley."

Luke had figured as much, since they were already late.

A group of parents and some of the medical staff from the children's ward had planned a picnic to celebrate Ben's birthday, a patient of Doctor Liam's. It had been a hard struggle for the past two months, but Ben had made it to fourteen. It was a day to rejoice, and everyone had assembled at the dock for a barbeque and boat rides up and down the river.

The traffic was fairly light as Mother made her way along the winding road that led to the bridge. Suddenly there was a loud bang, and the van swerved. Mother hung on tightly to the wheel, and pulled onto the shoulder of the road just before the entrance to the bridge.

"What happened?" Luke asked. "It sounded like a gunshot."

"More like a blown tire," Mother said. "Blasted construction sites and all their garbage. They're always doing something to this bridge."

She undid her coat from around her waist and pushed her arms into the sleeves, wrapping the nylon belt around her middle and tying it into a tight knot. She pushed open the doors and jumped out. The windshield wipers slapped rhythmically at the rain on the front window.

Luke watched from inside as she pulled out the tire and the tire iron from the back. He felt the van move as the air from passing vehicles rocked it. He couldn't see Mother anymore, but he could hear her working outside, changing the tire. It wasn't her first time; she had become quite mechanically inclined, thanks to all the things that typically went wrong with the van.

Luke grabbed his jacket off the seat and put it on. Maybe he could be of help. He checked David's straps, to be on the safe side, then gave his brother a rub on the head. "I'll be back in a minute," he said.

He slid into the passenger seat, exited out the door, and made his way to Mother's side. "Are you almost done?" he asked.

"I'm getting there," she said, as she removed the lug wrench from the tire after tightening it.

Luke was standing behind her, close to the embankment, when he heard the sudden warning of a loud and long horn blast. His blood froze as he saw a truck sliding toward them, hydroplaning through the water. He jumped back just before the vehicle collided with the back of the van. The impact brushed Smog up against Mother and shot her backwards into the grass at the edge of the shoulder. At the same time, the van was thrust forward into traffic, where it was hit three more times, the third collision driving it forward onto the bridge and into the cement guard rail. The barricade crumbled, and the van leaned forward, like a great green dragon hanging onto the edge of a precipice before flying away.

Luke stared at the van through the rain. People got out of their cars and rushed to see what they could do, while traffic backed up in all directions. Someone tried to talk to him, but he stumbled forward, moving toward their wrecked vehicle.

Was David in the van? He couldn't remember. He didn't want him to be in the van.

People milled around the van, trying to figure out what to do, afraid it would go over the side if they touched it.

Where is Mother? He forced his brain to think. Was she in the van? No, she wasn't there. His brain recalled her standing at the back tire just before the crash. His insides heaved, and he tried to work out if she had been hit or thrown clear. With tears in his eyes, he turned around again, and saw a group of people gathered near the side of the road. Suddenly Mother appeared, staggering through the crowd, looking disoriented and confused. There was a bleeding gash on the side of her head. She stumbled to the road, stopping to pick up the tire iron as she tried to make sense of her surroundings.

Relieved she was alive, and terrified that David wasn't, Luke broke into sobs and dropped to his knees.

Mother started toward him, tears of relief in her eyes. The moment dissolved when she saw the van. Still holding the tire iron, she changed her direction and started to jog. Luke heard a metallic moaning. The green van tipped farther forward.

Mother flew past Luke in a full run, sprinting toward the back of the van, where the ladder extended from the roof to the bottom of the doors. Her son was still inside. It was as if she and David were attached to the same cord, and if one was going over, the other would follow. It wasn't a conscious choice but autonomic, like both eyes moving together.

She shoved the tire iron in the front of her coat belt and twisted it. She didn't dare look at Luke as she ran past him; otherwise, she would have stopped. She kept her eyes on the van as it wavered. The crowd, not certain whether anyone was inside, moved away from the tottering monstrosity.

Luke watched Mother jump at the ladder on the back of the van, slotting the tire iron into the space between the rungs to hold herself secure. Her wet hair was in her face as she looked back at him. It was a moment that said everything and nothing.

Then the van pitched forward, and she and his brother were gone.

Chapter 45
Watching (2002)

At Dr. Liam's Celebration of Life, Luke rose from his chair to exercise his wandering mind by mingling for a while. He was tired of sitting and waiting. It wasn't that he didn't appreciate what Dr. Liam's family was doing, but he wanted to get it over with and go home. He stood by the gate and shyly chatted with one of the nurses from the practice.

A hospital van pulled up, and his heart skipped a beat. His anxiety lessened when the caregiver climbed out of the vehicle. "Ach, it took us longer than expected," she said in a Scottish brogue. "We had a few hiccups, so t' speak. The hospital weren't keen on letting us oot."

"It started a while ago," Luke said. He pulled open the side doors for the wheelchair lift.

"Aye. I know about how your mum always felt about being late, but it couldna be avoided. All the other vans were in use."

The wheelchair lift came to life, and Luke watched as the chair was loaded from inside the van, then locked into place. The lift lowered, and the sun shone on the head of the passenger, bringing a sparkle to the mass of blonde curls. His green eyes shone bright in such light, but there was a dullness to them on this day.

Luke undid the strap from the front of the lift when it reached the ground. "David! We've been waiting for you."

He waited until the lift came to a stop before positioning himself behind David's chair and pushing him forward. A portable IV pole stood beside him, with a line running into his arm. He also had a cast on one leg.

The Scottish nurse appeared alongside them with a bag of necessities for the day. She hooked it onto the back of the chair. "Where is she?"

"Inside, using the phone, I guess," replied Luke. "Does David get to come home with us soon?"

"I'd imagine he'll be discharged on Monday. Been a bit of a go for him, poor wee lad." She put a hand on David's arm. "It's almost time to send you home with your family," she said to him.

David looked back at her without expression. Then he looked into the crowd, searching for faces he recognized. He groaned softly, feeling more emotional than physical discomfort.

"What's the matter, pet?" the nurse asked. "What do you need, David?"

He felt startled by her question. What did he need? He needed something to hug.

The nurse looked away from David's face. "Do you think he knows what's going on?" she asked.

"He knows exactly what's going on," Luke said.

He heard his name called from farther down the sidewalk. The smallish figure of Mrs. Liam approached them. Her eyes showed sadness, but there was an unyielding strength behind them. She carried something in her hands that he recognized as Spike, the stuffed hedgehog that David had gifted to Dr. Liam for saving his life so many times. David's demeanor brightened when he caught sight of the stuffed animal cradled in her arm.

Chapter 46
Rescuing

Dr. Liam was taking the life jackets out of the boat at the dock when he saw it.

His family and staff had been celebrating an important birthday for his patient. They had spent their time on several activities, including feeding the ducks, cooking hotdogs on the open fire, and boating up and down the river. Then he heard the crash, and saw a van hanging over the edge of the bridge. The other guests gathered around, and he sent someone to call the authorities.

No one knew what to expect, but Dr. Liam readied one of the boats in case it was needed. Before he had it away from the dock, the van started to move. With everyone else, he watched in horror as it tipped forward, silently falling through the air before its impact with the river below.

His oldest daughter asked, "Honestly. You're not going out there, are you, Dad?"

"The boat is right here. There's no harm in checking." Deep down he felt sure it was useless, but in the end, hope is all there is.

He fired up the boat and sped toward the floating van, leaving his family watching.

* * *

When the van went over, Mother tucked her head into her arms, hoping that when she hit the water it would not knock her senseless. She felt fear, uncertainty, and timelessness. It seemed to take forever to fall into the river. She expected it to be like hitting a brick wall, but the distance from the bridge to the water wasn't that far, and the impact wasn't as severe as anticipated. She thought the van would sink quickly because of its weight, but the wheelchair lift balanced it at the centre, keeping it afloat for the time being.

She was still intact, so she unhitched herself from the ladder, holding the tire iron in her hand, and climbed the remaining rungs to the top of the van, thinking it might be easier to go in through the front window. She slid on her belly across the roof, trying to manage the shifts of the van's movements in the water without losing her balance and sliding into the river. Her adrenalin was running high and her senses felt sharp.

At the front of the roof, she swung the tire iron into the window glass to smash it, and it succumbed willingly. She dropped herself down onto the ledge of the windshield, her knees shaking with exertion, and crawled over the console, over the seat, and onto the floor. Her eyes searched the dark for her son, but she saw and heard nothing.

Chapter 47
Saving

Eternity passed as Mother steadied herself in the rocking van, trying to clear her head, waiting for her eyes to adjust to the darkness. Then she heard it, a soft "Hiiii," followed by a raptor noise and a whistle.

She wanted to fall to her knees at the sound. "David! It's OK. Mommy's here!"

She advanced her body in the direction of the sound, and collided with his chair. Her thoughts raced. If she got him out, then what? How would she support him in the current of the river and still get to shore? She ran her hands over his body, quickly undoing straps and speaking calm, comforting words while her mind searched for a way to float him in the water.

Suddenly she remembered the swimming items they kept in the back of the van. *Oh, please, Luke, please tell me you were the bad son and didn't take them out when I told you to!*

Crawling on her knees, she clawed at the floor for life jackets or floatation devices. She found one flipper, a mask, and a jacket. She scrambled her way back to David, and began putting him into the life jacket. Of his dozen or more straps, his waist buckle was the only one still engaged to keep him in his chair. She could hear the rustle of his hair against the leather of the headrest as he turned his head in search of her. He didn't seem in any distress, and let out a satisfied sigh. She knew he put all his trust and faith in her to rescue him, like she had done so many times before when he got sick. He looked relaxed and calm, doing his part by simply waiting. He made whistling sounds and his Chewbacca call to reassure her he was fine.

By the time she had snapped him into his lifejacket, the van was lower in the water. It had been only minutes since she entered. Water began to run in from the front windowsill, over the console and onto the floor. She held a shaking hand against David's chest to support him upright as she explained what they had to do. The easiest way to get him out was to wait for the water to rise to them, like they did at the pool, before floating him out the front window. But she wasn't sure how long he could hold his breath.

The water rose quickly. She pressed the button on the strap to release his waist, pulling him free of the chair. She thought of Luke, alone, waiting for his mother and brother, who had been devoured by the great green beast. She fought desperation, panic, and an overwhelming sense of guilt.

She waited until the water rose a bit more, then slid David from the chair. It all happened so fast. The water swelled into the cavity in one motion. She barely had time to shout, "Hold your breath!" Then she grabbed the front of his jacket, and scissor-kicked her legs toward the front window to drag him out.

As they almost cleared the front window, his sandal caught on the edge of the rearview mirror. She grabbed at the shoe and tried to wrench it free. Her air was near exhaustion, but she was able to get his foot out of the shoe, although she had pulled his leg hard in the process and felt something give. As the green dragon dropped into the depths of the water, she scrambled to get them to the surface.

Both their heads shot out of the water, and she inhaled air hungrily to fill her lungs. David was choking. She hung onto him, struggling to keep herself upright, not knowing how she was going to get them both to shore. They were being dragged along by the current, and she wrapped herself tightly around him, using the buoyancy provided by his lifejacket to keep her afloat. She didn't know much about undertow, but felt the best thing to do was to go with the current.

They bobbed in the water like a pair of corks. David continued to cough.

There was something blocking their path. She focused on it and realized it was an anchored boat, sitting sideways, rocking in the current. She struggled to hang onto David. They were racing toward the side of the boat. They were going to crash into it.

She tried to turn herself so that she would hit it first. She braced herself for the impact, turning her back in an attempt to shield her son. As she smashed against the boat, the force knocked the air out of her, but she hung on to David, reaching up with one arm, scrambling to find something to grasp to prevent herself from being pulled underneath.

A hand grabbed her arm, and her fingers found a hold and gripped the rim of the boat. The water pressed against her with amazing force and she couldn't move, but she could feel David slipping from her. She still had a tight grip on his life jacket, and she felt his limp body being slowly pulled up and away from her, into the boat.

An immense relief ran through her—and then a violent shaking gripped her. She felt too weak to keep her grip on the boat. Her body was being played with by the current, trying to force her downstream. She listened for the sounds of her son as she felt the river tugging at her to let go. She fought, but it was too strong. Her grip gave way and the river claimed her.

As she was torn away from the side of the boat, she caught sight of Dr. Liam forcing air into David's lungs to get him breathing again. She saw him pumping on David's chest in an effort to restart his heart.

She felt light as her body sped away from the vessel that held her son and her hope for survival, but she felt a sense of contentment and finality. She glanced up at the bridge, where she knew Luke was safe, and a joy filled her. Luke, her wonderful son, whose growth was so entwined with the roots and solidarity of his older brother. They operated as one, each giving to the other unconditionally, and with so much love.

She closed her eyes and stopped struggling. In the back of her mind, she heard the sound of a motor boat coming in her direction. She simply waited.

Chapter 48
Honouring

~~~~~~~

$\mathcal{D}r.$ Liam's yard was densely crowded, making it difficult for Luke to get David to the seating area. But he found a spot at last, and tucked the chair to the side so it didn't block the aisle. He made sure he had an extra seat beside him for her.

They fixed their attention on the flat screen; a familiar face flashed onto it. Norma, a seventeen-year-old girl with Down syndrome, had died of complications unrelated to her condition. She had been a patient of Dr. Liam's for most of her young life. A blissful smile and a look of pride filled her face. She wore a green-and-gold tracksuit with a Special Olympics medal pinned to her chest.

Her full name was announced, and her parents held hands as they walked to the front of the tent, toward the table arranged with candles and orchids. They took time to settle their anxiousness before returning their eyes to the screen to take in the photo of their daughter.

The mother attempted to speak but emotion overwhelmed her, and she leaned against her husband for support. He choked back tears before he spoke.

"You never know how much you're going to miss someone till they leave you," he said. "I must confess, we were concerned about how we would care for Norma when she was born, how she would be treated and how we would cope. Our fears got in our way at first, and we weren't sure we could do it. But she taught us how to go ignore our fears and to simply love her. Our girl was a bright star and her zest for life rubbed off on anyone who gave her a chance to shine. Our lives changed when she joined us, and our lives changed when she left us. We miss her terribly, but are thankful for our time together. We miss you so much, our darling baby girl."

Tears flowed freely among the crowd, and the couple was applauded for sharing their story. Each family who had lost a loved one had the opportunity to talk about their loss and their love for the person dear to them. The day was emotionally charged, and everyone became a part of everyone else's family through the sharing of stories.

Luke looked at David to see if the open emotion had affected him. But David's attention was elsewhere. His curly head turned toward the familiar sound of June's softly tinkling bells. He had a smile ready for when she came into view.

Her long hair swung softly as she knelt in front of David's chair. She rested one hand on Luke's knee in a form of greeting, and gave him a loving smile. "Sorry that took so long," she said. "I was on the phone trying to find out where David was, and I see we found him. So happy to see you, David! How are you feeling?"

He twittered like a bird, and finished his remarks with what sounded like a raptor. He fanned his hand through the scarf that hung around her neck, bringing the bells to life again.

"I see," June said. Then she looked at Luke. "I hope I haven't missed it."

He shook his head.

She sat in the chair next to Luke and scanned the audience, feeling the bond of shared pain. In one sense, it was a way to experience and own the grief; in another, it was overwhelming, since the tears never seemed to stop. They flowed from one story to the next, creating a river, a lake, and finally an ocean. Staying afloat had its difficulties, but the process remained meaningful.

She watched Dr. Liam approach the podium. He held the microphone and looked at the screen, ready to announce the next name. A number of orchids and candles were missing from the table at this point. June bowed her head in thanks to the family who did so much for so many souls, and for their efforts to recognize the importance and impact of all of these lives. Then she raised her head as the face of her beloved friend appeared on the screen.

Chapter 49
Speaking

June stood, glancing down at Luke, whose eyes were leaking tears. She slid past David into the aisle, and the boys got ready to follow her. Her limbs felt heavy as she walked forward to the front of the table.

She looked at the screen where Mother smiled back at her from a photo taken at the water park with Luke and David. All three were caught in laughter. The boys were in their swim suits, while Mother wore shorts and a T-shirt that sported the word "muggle" on the front. June smiled, then turned to address the crowd.

"I am here to honour a person who lost her life in an effort to save her child. I know that she wouldn't want me to talk about how fierce her love for her children was, or how devoted she was to her boys. Parents are like that. She would want me to talk about how children are our driving force, and how our love for them changes us, molds us, and makes us better. She would have said we learn so much from our children that we often feel like the child. This day is filled with extraordinary parents grieving the loss of their beloved children and who must now adjust to change. Change is difficult and painful, but we all manage when we support one another and hold strong."

She was about to return the microphone to Dr. Liam, but in a moment of inspiration, held it out to Luke instead. Much to her surprise, he took it.

He spoke timidly into it at first, testing the sound, but soon found his voice. "I just want to say I miss my mom. Her name is Edurne, but my dad used to call her Eddie. Sometimes she made me feel great and sometimes I felt like I didn't matter to her at all. I believed I wasn't worth anything because out of all of the stuff we did? . . . it never seemed to be about me. But my brother showed me something I hadn't noticed before. It's not about how perfect your life seems, but how well you can give and receive joy. Making others happy can make you happy. And what makes me the happiest is my family. My mom helped me figure that out."

Luke hesitated a moment to take a calming breath. "We will never stop loving you, Mom. We miss you more than you can imagine, and will think of you every day for the rest of our lives."

Teary-eyed, he turned the microphone back to Dr. Liam, who gave him a long lighter with a white handle in return. Luke chose a candle from the table, and held it in front of his brother. Together, hand-over-hand, they lit the flame, and Luke returned it to the table. The flames from all the candles flickered in unison and grew, as though offering the crowd a signal that said, "Remember us."

Luke placed the lighter on the table's edge, positioned himself behind David's chair, and pushed him toward their seats by the aisle. June joined them, and sat beside them in respectful silence.

Chapter 50
Releasing

A break was announced to allow people to stretch their legs and move around. Everyone was invited to the "green space," which was a vacant lot next door that had been turned into a park-like area by the local community. There was freshly mowed grass on a landscape that included a small hill. A few trees, some wild rose bushes, and a large bed of pansies had been planted along one border. The crowd from the driveway moved into the area, and June pushed David's chair across the grass to a place near the hill.

Luke joined the crowd watching a group of young girls in long, gossamer-like dresses standing on the hill. They looked like fairies, or angels, or wood sprites. Music began playing, and the girls moved to the song that spilled out into the afternoon air. He recognized Colleen among the dancers. The music stopped; she smiled in his direction and waved.

He heard Dr. Liam's whistle, and turned to see him approaching. David swung his head back, craning his neck to see the person attached to the familiar sound. Dr. Liam crouched in front of his chair, placed a large hand onto his knee, and shook him. "I've been looking for you," he said gently. "How are you, David?"

"All seems well," June said. "He should be coming home soon, I believe?"

"Yes, he's close. Maybe tomorrow. Hey! I see a thief!" he said teasingly, and tried to pull Spike free from David's grip.

David held on tighter, showing no intention of letting go.

"I do recall you gave him to me," Dr. Liam said good-humouredly. "But you can hold him for a bit. I want him back, though."

He stood and looked at Luke. "I know it was hard, but you gave a lovely tribute to your mother," he said.

Luke couldn't find words to answer, and simply nodded.

"Well," said Dr. Liam, "my wife has come up with yet another wonderful way of symbolically acknowledging our loved ones and demonstrating how much they mean to us. Wait and watch. I think you'll enjoy it." He placed a kiss on each boy's forehead, then moved through the crowd, stopping to chat as he walked.

Luke's attention returned to the field, where he saw Mrs. Liam directing a few men holding wooden crates. The crowd gathered as the crates were set side by side on the ground. The sun shone warmly as it had all morning, and a ray of bright light settled on the top of a box. One of the keepers pulled on a door at the front of the crate, and a cloud of white doves emerged from inside, spilling into the light. The second crate was opened, and more white doves fluttered into the air. The sound of their wings and the sight of them as they flew upward drew gasps from the crowd.

Luke shielded his eyes to follow the birds, circling high overhead as though searching for heaven. They eventually flew out of sight, and he dropped a hand onto his brother's shoulder. Everyone moved back towards the house, and he followed with David and June. He felt grateful that the day to honour and remember Mother and the lives of family lost had not yet ended, and would be forever cherished.

Epilogue

~~~

June came in through her back gate; the boys and Colleen followed. They had gone for a bike ride around the block and enjoyed the happiness it had given them.

Rayne sat at the picnic table in the back yard. The otherwise tidy yard was now cluttered with toys and the boys' paraphernalia. "How did it go?" he asked.

"It was fantastic!" Luke said. "David's bike is the best thing ever!"

He dropped his bike on the grass and moved to his brother's side. David was seated in a recumbent bike made especially for him. It allowed him to partially lie back, with his feet strapped to the pedals. The rest of his body was tied in with straps that allowed him to move while remaining supported inside the frame. When the bike was pushed from behind, the pedals rotated, and David's legs, strapped to the pedals, followed. It gave him fresh-air and exercise; he was thrilled and loved the bike.

June stood beside Rayne, leaning into him with happy tears in her eyes. "I think I'll make some iced tea and get snacks out for the kids."

"Let me help," Colleen offered. She followed June inside.

"Snacks? What kind of snacks?" Rayne asked, rising out of his chair. "Do we have any of those ice cream thingies that look like big cookies?" The screen door shut behind him with a bang.

Luke realized their alone time would be limited now. Since they'd moved in with June and Rayne, he and David were seldom by themselves. Nothing much got past June, and they were kept under a pretty close eye. The authorities were still making efforts to locate their dad, but had granted foster rights to June and Rayne until the legalities were sorted out.

With a moment to themselves, Luke looked over David's bike, generously funded by an organization that helped children with disabilities. It was well built and he wondered...

"How fast do you think this can go?" he asked his brother.

"Ahhh?" David said, sounding concerned.

"No really, I wonder how fast this could actually go."

He looked around. A delivery van was parked at the edge of the property, left running by the driver, who had walked to a door further up the street.

"Come on," Luke said. He picked up a long skipping rope and headed for the back of the van, pushing David along with him. "I'll hold on behind you on my skateboard when we take off."

He tied the front of the bike to the handle on the back door of the van, before grabbing his board from the side of the lawn.

David screeched in fear. The driver would return any second, and with the sound of the motor, it was doubtful anyone would hear his screams. There was no hope of escape ... until he heard the sweet jingling of bells getting louder.

End

About the Author

Gwenyth Snow lives in Edmonton, Alberta, Canada. She worked as a Licensed Practical Nurse for nearly twenty years before deciding to change her profession. In her late thirties she attended the University of Alberta and achieved a Bachelor of Arts degree in English and an after degree in Education. During that time, she became enchanted by so many of the books that she read, that she developed an interest in writing. In addition to writing and teaching at an elementary school, she has a passion for film and travel. This is her first novel.

https://gwen3315.wixsite.com/mysite

Printed in Canada